"I wish you needed my help, Rae."

Nick McKenzie looked directly at her as he spoke. "It makes me feel guilty asking you to help me with *my* problem when there seems to be nothing I can do for you."

"You have a problem?" Rae murmured.

He nodded. "My son. Kevin."

She put down her wineglass, looking surprised and somewhat alarmed. Then she reached across the table to touch his hand. "Mr. McKenzie, I assure you—"

"Nick."

"Nick. I assure you that any problem Kevin has is mine, too. While he's living with my family, I feel absolutely responsible for him. So whatever's wrong, please tell me."

Nick sighed. "The problem is really mine. One I haven't been able to solve for twelve years."

"Oh?"

"My son hates me."

Eva Rutland began writing when her four children, now all successful professionals, were growing up. She has become a regular—and very popular—contributor to Harlequin's Romance and Regency series. Eva lives in California with her husband, Bill, who actively supports and encourages her writing career.

Books by Eva Rutland

HARLEQUIN ROMANCE
2897—TO LOVE THEM ALL
2944—AT FIRST SIGHT
3064—NO ACCOUNTING FOR LOVE
3240—ALWAYS CHRISTMAS

HARLEQUIN REGENCY ROMANCE
1—MATCHED PAIR
20—THE VICAR'S DAUGHTER
28—ENTERPRISING LADY
45—THE WILLFUL LADY
89—GRETNA BRIDE

FOREIGN AFFAIR
Eva Rutland

Harlequin Books

TORONTO • NEW YORK • LONDON
AMSTERDAM • PARIS • SYDNEY • HAMBURG
STOCKHOLM • ATHENS • TOKYO • MILAN
MADRID • WARSAW • BUDAPEST • AUCKLAND

ISBN 0-373-03283-8

Harlequin Romance first edition October 1993

FOREIGN AFFAIR

CHAPTER ONE

RAE PASCAL RUSHED down the hospital corridor, filled with dread. *Dear God, don't let it be serious!* A lump rose in her throat as she thought of Kevin, the quiet sober English boy who had already stolen her heart, although he'd been with them a scant two weeks.

And now... When she'd called the hospital, the report had been sketchy. An accident, she was told. Thrown from his bicycle. He was apparently somewhat disoriented, but the extent of his injuries wasn't fully determined. He'd been brought in three hours ago and was still in Emergency. Oh, poor Kevin, hurt, frightened and surrounded by strangers! And she hadn't been here! *Disoriented.* A cold chill swept through her. Dear God, please, let it not be serious, she prayed, as a web of guilt closed around her. Of all the days to be out of town! She quickened her steps, haunted by her mother's warning.

"A foreign exchange student! You must be out of your mind! And only how old? Sixteen! Really, Rae, as if you didn't have enough to handle with your own two boys!"

It's my fault, she thought. *But I didn't expect anything like this to happen. Oh, poor Kevin. I should have been here.* Almost overwhelmed by the guilt and dread, she brushed past a tall man standing near the admittance desk.

"Kevin McKenzie," she told the clerk, her voice hoarse. "Is he—Where—How is he?"

"McKenzie." The clerk punched the name into the computer. "He's in X-ray, ma'am."

"But he's—" Rae's throat felt dry and she could hardly speak. "He's okay, isn't he? I mean—"

"You'll have to talk with Dr. Langston. He'll be out shortly."

"Oh." Of course the clerk couldn't tell her anything. That didn't necessarily mean the worst. *Please, God, please let him be all right.*

"I got here as soon as I could. You see, I was out of town and didn't get your message until..." No need to go into that. "You'll need this," she said, her fingers trembling as she reached into the smart leather bag that swung from her shoulder. "I have his medical card and insurance."

"It's all right, ma'am." The clerk looked at her with sympathy. "Everything's been taken care of."

"Oh." But how? His mother was in England. Surely... "You've notified his mother?" she asked through parched lips.

"Oh, I don't think that will be necessary." The husky voice came from behind her and she wheeled around.

"You're the doctor? Is Kevin—"

"No, but I've talked with Dr. Langston. He thinks it's only a slight concussion. They're running some tests just to be sure."

"I see." But she wasn't relieved and could not stop trembling.

"We'll just have to wait. Why don't you sit here?" The man spoke with concern as he took her arm and led her to a chair. Dimly she was aware that he was tall, that he wore a sports shirt and slacks, and spoke with a lilting, somewhat foreign accent. Scottish? Why was he here?

She sat down, then stood up again as a thought jolted her. Had it been this man's car that hit Kevin? "Did—Were you—I mean, you saw the accident?"

"No, I got here about an hour ago. I'm Kevin's father."

"Pardon?" She must have misunderstood.

"I'm Nick McKenzie, Kevin's father."

"But I thought..." She stopped. It was hardly polite to tell a man you thought he was dead. Not once in all those mountains of paper had there been any reference to a father; not once had Kevin mentioned him. A mother and stepfather, Lord and Lady Fraser, with whom Kevin lived in London. McKenzie grandparents in Scotland. Yes. That was it. Scottish. Quite different from Kevin's precise English tongue.

Father? He'd been nonexistent until this very moment. Maybe she should ask for some identification. She felt an hysterical desire to laugh—or to cry. And how had he managed to get here before she did? From England? Scotland? And just out of the blue when something had happened to Kevin. Kevin!

"Only a slight concussion?" she asked anxiously. "Have you seen him? Do you think...?"

"Now, we'll not be thinking the worst, Mrs.... Pascal, isn't it?"

She nodded, wondering how he knew who she was. And, if so, why did he look surprised? She brushed the thought aside. Nothing mattered but the boy who had been in her care less than a month. Fear and guilt riveted her to the spot.

"He's a bit dazed, after taking such a blow. And with no helmet, foolish lad. But he'll come round," the man said firmly, and she wondered if he was trying to reassure himself or her.

"What happened?" she asked.

"Come. Let's get out of here and I'll tell you what I know."

Rae had hardly been aware of the other people in the reception area, a man with a rasping cough, a woman sitting quietly knitting, a fretting baby. But she allowed him to lead her out of the room and into the relative quiet of a long corridor. There, they paced up and down as he told her as much as he'd been able to find out. According to the police report, Kevin, to avoid hitting a dog, had swerved from the bicycle lane directly into a truck.

"Thank God it was moving slowly, but it was a heavy rigger and..." The man spread his hands. "Well, he took quite a fall, broke his arm and—"

"Oh, no!"

"Don't be distressed. It's easy to set a broken arm."

"Yes." She knew and he knew that wasn't the major concern. The concussion was. "I hope it's not—" She tried to pull herself together, tried to stop shaking. "But if they thought it necessary to notify you, it must mean—"

"No, no, nothing like that!" he said in a rallying tone. "It was just that they couldn't treat him without some authority and when they couldn't find you or his mother..." He shrugged. "Jan and Lord Fraser are traveling in Australia, you know. So they phoned my folks in Scotland, who called me. Luckily I was here."

She stared at him, trying to sort it all out. This man—she hadn't even known he existed... "You were *here?*"

"Well, nearby. At Pebble Beach."

She stared at him. He had been here in the States. Vacationing at Pebble Beach. And had made no attempt to contact his son? Obviously one of those absentee fathers who never bothered to even keep in touch, never bothered to call or write, let alone visit.

He smiled, seemingly unaware of her contempt. "Luckily I managed to charter a plane and flew right up. As a matter of fact, I had planned to come up to pay Kevin a visit next week. Thought I'd surprise him."

And surprise me too, Rae thought. So he'd planned to visit, had he? A sneaky unexpected visit, probably to check up on her. And by what right? she thought as a sudden rage possessed her. So distant from his son that not once in two whole weeks had Kevin mentioned that he *had* a father! But then her defensive rage crumpled as she thought of the injured boy. She hadn't been here when he needed her.

"I'm so sorry I was out of town! Oh, I should have been here!" she cried, almost to herself. But the meeting at Modesto, two hours away, hadn't been over until five. She'd left immediately, never even considering Jack Weston's invitation to dinner. Even so, by the time she'd picked up Joey and stopped by the grocery... It was after nine when she got the message on her answering machine.

"I thought the boys would be okay until I got home," she said aloud, feeling the need to explain to someone, even this man who didn't deserve an explanation. "Joey, my ten-year-old, was with a sitter. Greg had a game tonight and I thought Kevin would be with him. The games are never over before nine, you see, and usually the boys..." She knew she was rambling but couldn't stop the flow of words. "Usually, you see, they go out for burgers after the game and I thought Kevin... Oh, it's all my fault! I never thought he'd be on his bike during rush hour!"

"Hush." He took both her hands in his. "Stop blaming yourself. As my grandfather always said, The wind blows, the water flows, and the one has little to do with the other."

His lilting voice somehow calmed her, and she stared up at him. "That may be true," she said thoughtfully, "but in this case—"

"In this case, it's definitely true," he assured her. "You were about *your* business and Kevin was about his." She started to protest but he lifted his hand to check her. "Kevin is not a child. He's sixteen, almost a man, and I'll lay you a bet that even had you been home and not on some important business of your own, Kevin would still have been on his bike. Probably headed toward the library... or maybe to the veterinary college. And—" his mouth twisted wryly "—the foolish lad would always risk his own safety for any animal in his path."

He was trying to comfort her. She was strangely touched and for the first time studied the man. Between thirty-five and forty, she guessed. A craggy, not conventionally handsome face. Deeply tanned, with very thick, very black hair, and eyes of the deepest blue she had ever seen. Warm understanding eyes.

"Thank you," she said, drawn by the warmth. "I guess I just have a guilt complex. My mother said I shouldn't have taken on the extra responsibility. I'm single, you see. My husband died soon after Joey was born.''

"I'm sorry. That must have been hard on you."

"Yes," she answered, flushing from an even greater guilt. She had told no one, not even her mother, about the talk she and Tom had had the day before his heart attack. But Nick McKenzie was right; it *had* been hard. She'd moved back with her parents, and it had been good for the boys, being with her dad. She knew they felt doubly deprived when he'd died, three years ago. "I was approached last year about taking a foreign exchange student, and I thought, well why not! We have lots of room." She'd been happy for her mother when she had married again the year before and moved to Oregon. But Rae had felt so alone, with her mother gone, and the weight of her responsibility seemed heavier. "I thought another male in the house..." She paused. "No, the truth is it was for a very selfish reason. My Greg, a year younger than Kevin, is a good kid, but his heart's on the basketball court, or rather the football field this time of year. Anyway, definitely not on books. So I thought having a peer around, a boy with academic standards like Kevin's might be a good influence."

He smiled at her but shook his head. "Like mixing oil and water."

"Oh, no, Greg and Kevin get along beautifully," she protested, then hesitated. Greg had been on the football field while Kevin headed for the university library. "Maybe it *wasn't* such a good idea," she reflected in a low voice. "And certainly I had a selfish motive."

"Which gives Kevin the opportunity to attend a private American high school with excellent standards.

Not to mention that this high school isn't far from the world-famous Dansby School of Veterinary Medicine. He plans to be a veterinarian, as you've no doubt already discovered. No, whatever your motive, I'm sure Kevin considers it a favor.''

"I hope he still thinks so," she said ruefully. "It's taking so long. Do you think—''

"It takes time to set an arm," he told her, again ignoring the possibility of a serious head injury. "Not to worry. I'm thinking Kevin will weather this better than yourself. Can I get you something? A cup of coffee?''

"No, thank you." But she was grateful for his offer. She glanced at him, noticing for the first time his casual but expensive attire. Gucci loafers, well-fitting slacks, Polo shirt. As smart and fashionably correct for vacationing at Carmel, she supposed, as her dark-green gabardine coatdress was for a business meeting. And he seemed so relaxed. *He might still be on the beach instead of waiting to see if his son is in a coma,* she thought with some irritation. She shook her head slightly; she was being unfair. He was here, wasn't he?

"A strange way for us to meet," he remarked, smiling, and she noticed the way his cheeks creased, softening his face and making him appear almost handsome. "But I expect we'll be seeing a good deal of each other.''

"Perhaps," she said dubiously and was irked by the tiny spark of pleasure evoked by the possibility. She knew about absentee fathers. Anyway, there was no room in her life for a man. And how could she even be thinking about it while Kevin—

"Mr. McKenzie?''

Rae's heart gave a little thump as she saw the nurse approach. The man beside her stiffened and stark terror was reflected in his face. All that "Kevin will come round" had been to allay her own fears. As they followed the nurse to the consultation room, Rae knew that McKenzie was as apprehensive as she. She saw his anxious gaze focus on Kevin and sensed in him the same overwhelming surge of relief that swept through her. Kevin's left arm was in a cast and he looked wan, but definitely alert.

"So, my son! How're you feeling?" There was a tremor in McKenzie's voice.

"Dad! You're here?" Kevin's obvious surprise held a flash of genuine delight.

"Of course I'm here. With you scaring your grandma half to death?" McKenzie brushed back a lock of hair that had fallen over Kevin's forehead. He did it so carefully, Rae thought, almost as if he were afraid to touch his own son.

Kevin looked a little embarrassed. "I didn't mean to—Well, it was this dog. He ran right out in front of me and...I think I hit him. Did I?"

"I...I don't know." McKenzie looked at the doctor.

"There was some mention of a dog in the police report," Dr. Langston confirmed. "But only in reference to your avoiding him. That's what caused the accident. Lucky you were sideswiped and not hit head-on."

"I'll say you were lucky." McKenzie's face clouded with anger. "You should never swerve out of the bicycle path! Bashed yourself up proper, didn't you?"

The delight she had seen in Kevin's eyes was so quickly masked that Rae wondered if she'd imagined it. She heard the boy mutter a sheepish, "Pretty clumsy of me, huh?"

"No. Just what I'd expect of you," McKenzie said, frowning. He turned to anxiously question the doctor and didn't notice his son's expression. Coupled with the pain Kevin was obviously feeling was an embarrassed little-boy look that made Rae want to take him in her arms and cuddle him as she would Joey.

"You'll soon be feeling better," she soothed, lightly rubbing his shoulder. "I know you've had a rough time. But you'll soon be home and in your own bed. Are you hungry?" He shook his head but the hurt-little-boy look did not go away, and Rae wished she could tell him, "He meant you'd never hurt a dog, not that you're clumsy." There was something here she couldn't fathom, a constraint between these two people who were so much alike. The same dark blue eyes and black hair, the same irregularity of features. How was it she hadn't noticed the resemblance the minute she saw Nick McKenzie?

All attention was now on the doctor as McKenzie bombarded him with questions. Once he was assured that the concussion was slight, all tests negative, and there was no internal bleeding, he concentrated on the broken arm. Was it a clean break? How long to heal? What precautions—

"Hold on." The doctor held up a hand and smiled. "Yes, I knew you'd be concerned about that, Nick McKenzie." The doctor spoke the name with a kind of familiarity and awe that made Rae wonder. Who was Nick McKenzie? She was even more puzzled at the doctor's next words. "Never thought to meet you in the flesh, sir. Saw that spectacular performance on television last Sunday. Great! Just great!''

"Thanks." McKenzie absently shook the doctor's hand. "But about this broken arm..."

"We're lucky," said Dr. Langston. "No fractures. An absolutely clean break." He then advised about medication and further treatment and Rae listened intently. After all, Kevin was in her charge.

When they left the doctor's office, McKenzie looked at his watch. "We should call the folks," he told Kevin. "So you can tell them yourself that you're still alive and kicking."

"Call from my house," Rae offered. It was now almost midnight, and she wanted to get Kevin to bed as soon as possible. He looked exhausted. "But perhaps..." She glanced at McKenzie. Perhaps he didn't intend to come by her house or even stay in town.

"Good idea," he said promptly. "Kevin can ride with me and I'll trail you."

Dansby was a small university town, and the drive from the hospital to her home a short one. Her mind, racing ahead, detouring, traversed a far greater distance.

The boys. Joey would have been bedded down with Helen's three kids, and since tomorrow was Saturday she'd just leave him there. Greg, always good about curfews, thank goodness, would be home now. He could help Kevin get undressed and into bed. Or perhaps Kevin's father would. Or would he just dump the boy and leave? Strange she'd never heard of him.

And strange how the doctor spoke to him, as if he was somebody important. And how casually McKenzie had accepted his obvious adulation, as if he was

accustomed to being fawned over. Must be famous for
something. And too busy being famous to be close to
his son. Well, *he* wasn't her business. Kevin was. The
doctor said to give him something hot before he went
to bed. Soup maybe. Poor kid. It had been a long day
for him.

Long day for her, too. The tedious drive there and
back. She could have driven up with the two other
bank officers from Sacramento, but they were staying
overnight and she had to get back to the boys. Tedious
business session, too. That branch was in trouble, big
trouble. Would have been nice to stay for a relaxing
dinner as Weston had suggested. No. She was glad she
was too busy to have to deal with the likes of Weston.

Lord, she was tired. The house was a wreck and
there'd be the usual wrangle about Saturday chores.
Greg had football practice at twelve. So he wouldn't be
around for Joey's birthday party at one. Thank goodness she'd scheduled it at Goosey Gander's Miniature
Golf Course. Still, the vision of fifteen wild ten-year-
olds romping roughshod through those neat nursery-
rhyme putting greens haunted her. Kevin had said he
would help, but now with his broken arm . . . Oh, well,
she'd tough it out. Anyway, Saturday was shot.

With luck, she'd have time Sunday to go over all that
merger data before Monday's staff meeting. Luck,
nothing! She wasn't about to be as unprepared as
Harrison Bowers, the new director, obviously expected her to be! Good thing she'd received her promotion before his appointment.

Good heavens! Home already? She got out of the
car, followed by Kevin and his father who had pulled
up behind her. She led them through the garage-door

entrance to the family room, fervently hoping that Greg hadn't left smelly football togs or sneakers in the middle of the floor.

"Hi, Mom!" Greg came hurrying toward them, turning on lights. "Hey, Kev, how're you—*Nick McKenzie?*"

McKenzie?"

CHAPTER TWO

IT WASN'T THE THING, Rae thought as she took down
a can of soup, to ask a man you'd just met who or what
he was. But she could hardly restrain herself. First the
doctor and now Greg. Greg, anxious about Kevin, had
waited up, but after his "Man, that's tough!" had
transferred his awed attention to McKenzie.

"How come you never told me he was your dad?"
he asked now, nodding toward the man on the phone.

"Thought you knew," Kevin answered, squirming
uneasily as if embarrassed by the connection.

"Come and tell your grandma you're all right."
McKenzie beckoned from the wall phone and Kevin
went to exchange a lively conversation with his Scottish grandparents. Their talk centered, as far as Rae
could determine, more on certain of the farm animals
than on his broken arm.

McKenzie stayed to see his son safely in bed and Rae
had no chance to be alone with Greg until he'd left.

"Greg," she said as soon as the door closed behind
him, "who is that man?"

"Mom! He's *Nick McKenzie!*"

"Thank you. I know his name."

"You must be kidding! I can't believe you don't
know who Nick McKenzie is."

"And *I* can't believe you left your sneakers in the middle of the floor again!" She picked them up and tossed them in his direction.

"Aw, Mom!" he groaned, just managing to catch them.

"Don't give me that! You leave a trail like a snail. I've told you and told you, if we'd just pick up... Oh, never mind," she said with a sigh of resignation. "Just tell me why everybody gawks at this man. Is he a movie star?" She hadn't been to a movie in years. She hardly had time for more than the news on television.

"Getting warm, Mom." Greg grinned at her. "He's primo, all right. Haven't you ever heard of McKenzie clubs?"

"Clubs?" Now she was completely mystified.

"Golf clubs. McKenzie signature clubs are tops."

"Oh, I see. He's a golf pro, huh?"

"He's the golf pros' pro, Mom! He holds a record of three PGA championships—back-to-back. Two Master's green coats. And right now he's competing in the Bing Crosby Clambake at Pebble Beach."

"I'm impressed." Not so much at Nick McKenzie's apparent fame, but her son's articulation of it. His usual comments consisted of grunts or monosyllables. Now he was rattling on like a sports commentator about golf, PGA's and green coats, whatever they were!

"I'll bet he withdrew," Greg said, shaking his head. "That's tough, 'cause he's always in the hunt."

"Hunt? What does that mean?"

"In the lead, Mom, in the lead! And leaving Pebble Beach means, like, he walked off from a hundred and fifty grand. Or, say he didn't make first, then he'd for sure be second or third and they rake in, like, maybe seventy-five or eighty thousand. Anyway, big bucks!"

A golf tournament. Not exactly a vacation. And that kind of money! "Just for playing golf?" she asked.

"You get about two grand if you just make the cut! And Nick McKenzie! Ma-a-n!" Greg scratched his ear with the toe of one sneaker. "And, like, he just cut out!"

"Maybe he'll just cut back in," Rae said, picking up one of Joey's shirts and a soccer ball. Hadn't he said something about chartering a plane to fly up here? Things had happened so fast tonight that it hadn't really registered. "If he's making that kind of money he can just fly back and—"

"Uh-uh, you can't do that. They're real fussy. No time out or anything like that. You're out if you miss your turn at play, even if you're two minutes late for your tee time."

"But this was an emergency," Rae argued, yawning. "And if he's the big shot you say he is, he'll work something out. Anyway, put these in Joey's room, and scram. Tomorrow's a big day and it's already here."

She was bone-tired. But she did like things tidy in the morning. She went back into the kitchen, cleared off the table and set out the breakfast dishes. She picked up the pan with the remains of chicken noodle soup. Was it enough to save or should she just dump it? The peal of the doorbell startled her and she almost dropped the saucepan.

Who on earth could it be at this hour? She moved cautiously to the door, then opened it a crack.

"It's Nick McKenzie, Mrs. Pascal. I found Kevin's dog."

"Kevin's dog?" She pulled the door wide, staring at him, and at the small animal in his arms.

"I'm sorry," he said hurriedly. "I know this is an imposition but I didn't know where to find a vet at this hour and I'm at a hotel—" he gestured helplessly "—so I thought if you could find a box and some newspapers..."

Suddenly aware that she was blocking the door, she stepped back. "Of course. Do come in. I'll see what I can find."

"Mother was right," she muttered to herself as she went into the garage. "I must have been out of my mind." But all she'd bargained for was a quiet academic-minded exchange student. She didn't expect him to run into a truck. And she hadn't asked for an injured dog! Certainly not now after the day she'd had! But she found a sturdy grocery carton and gathered up some newspapers, then hurried back in, trying to hide her irritation. This was too much!

But she couldn't help being touched by his tenderness as he laid the dog in the box, carefully straightening its legs. "Kevin was so worried," he explained. "He kept thinking he'd hit the dog. Wanted to stop when I brought him home. But Kevin needed to get to bed, so I wouldn't stop then. But I knew the dog was on his mind. So I went back to look for him."

"And he'd been there all this time?"

"I knew he would be if he was hurt. Animals often have more sense than humans do. They lie still and wait for nature to heal them. He'd crawled right under a bush."

"Poor little creature. Lying so quiet and patient for so long." She thought of the man searching in the dark. And he must be as tired as she. The dog, as if he understood, lay quiet and docile, large dark eyes fixed trustingly on his benefactor. Every now and then the tail gave a friendly twitch. Rae gently rubbed a finger along one ear, brushed a leaf from the grubby tangled coat. No collar. "Do you think he's badly hurt?"

"Don't know about internal injuries, but these two hind legs are definitely broken. I'll get him to a vet in the morning. Do you mind if I leave him here, just for tonight?"

"Of course he can stay here. Shouldn't I get him some water? An aspirin?" He wasn't making any noise but he must be in pain.

"Good idea. Maybe a scrap of bread and if you have any of that soup left..."

Nick McKenzie was a caring man, Rae thought later as she climbed wearily into bed. She had hardly remembered a dog. But he had. And he knew Kevin was worried and went back to look for him. She fell asleep thinking of strong gentle hands spooning crushed aspirin and water into the dog's mouth, dipping bread into soup and patiently holding it to the needy, trusting tongue.

MORNINGS WERE ALWAYS hectic, even on Saturdays. But the presence of the dog created even more chaos than usual, with Joey shouting, "A dog, Mom! Where'd you get him? You said we couldn't have another dog."

And she had meant that in the aftermath of the grieving when Taffy, their beautiful collie had been hit by a car a year ago. "He's not ours. Mr. McKenzie brought him because he's hurt and—"

"I hit him. I knew it. And Dad went back?" Kevin's eyes opened wide. "I wanted him to stop but he wouldn't."

"Because he knew you needed to get to bed. Don't pick him up, Joey."

"No, Joey, he's hurt. I think his leg is broken," Kevin said. "Maybe both of them."

"Let him stay quiet," Rae advised. "Wash your hands and come to breakfast."

But Kevin insisted that he attend to the dog first. Again she noticed the similarity to his father as he knelt and carefully spooned warm oatmeal into the dog's mouth.

The animal created such a distraction that she was glad when McKenzie arrived to pick him up. His eyes focused anxiously on Kevin. "How are you feeling?"

"Okay. Look, we can take him up to the college. I— I can show you the way," he offered hesitantly.

"Sure. Let's get going." McKenzie leaned down for the box.

"I'll go, too," Joey said eagerly, still in his pajamas.

"No, you won't," Rae intervened. "You haven't done your room yet. And you're not even dressed."

"I don't see why I have to work when today's my birthday."

"Because you also eat, sleep and bathe on your birthday," Rae answered.

McKenzie's mouth gave an amused quirk. "We'll take good care of him," he assured Joey.

"And you'll bring him right back? We are going to keep him, aren't we, Mom?"

They exchanged glances and McKenzie quickly came to her rescue. "We'd better leave him with the vet for a couple of weeks. To check him out, let him recover. Then you and your mom can decide."

At last they departed with the dog and she got the boys started on their chores. She didn't intend to have two healthy, lazy boys demanding hefty allowances while somebody else cleaned up after them.

As she stuffed towels into the washing machine, she listened to the hum of the lawnmower. There had been a bit of a skirmish but she'd won. She knew Greg missed Kevin, especially when it came to outdoor chores. She chuckled and began to load the breakfast dishes into the dishwasher. She had been told to treat her foreign student as one of the family. She found that Kevin, evidently accustomed to a staff of servants in London, didn't know the first thing about making his own bed. But he was a dynamo with outdoor work because, as he said, "I always help Grandpa at the farm." Before leaving for the vet, he'd said his arm wasn't troubling him at all and sure, he could still help with Joey's party. She hoped so. Kevin had a way with Joey and his friends, and they weren't an easy lot to handle.

Later, when the boys were getting cleaned up and she was giving the sink a last rinse, the doorbell rang. They were back. She took off her rubber gloves and went down the hall to open the door.

"No internal injuries," Nick reported.

"I'm glad," she said, noticing for the first time what a wonderful all's-right-with-the-world smile he had. "Come on back and have a cup of coffee."

"I'd like to take you and the boys out to lunch," he announced as he followed her into the kitchen. "I'm leaving early in the morning so I won't have another chance to—"

"Thank you, that's kind of you. But I'm sorry. I have a birthday party scheduled."

"And I promised to help," Kevin put in.

"Oh, no," said Rae. "Your father's only going to be here today. Go to lunch with him. I can manage."

When Kevin declared he wouldn't desert her, she turned to his father. "Perhaps you'd like to join us? If you can stand it, that is. The party's at this miniature golf course and . . ." Her voice trailed off before she added doubtfully, "Fifteen ten-year-olds at Goosey Gander's silly putting greens—I don't know if I can inflict that on you."

"I'd like to come. And perhaps I could be of help. After all, golf is my game."

"That would be great, Dad. You could take my place and I could go back up to the college." Kevin answered the question in both their faces. "I might have a job. That's where I was going last night. Dr. Williams said they needed someone to feed the small animals and clean the pens."

McKenzie winced. "All that muck? And with that arm? Wouldn't it be too hard on you?"

"No. It's just two hours twice a week." Kevin's expression had grown stubborn. "Dr. Williams practically promised I could have the job and I don't want to miss this chance." He turned to Rae. "If Dad will take over for me . . ."

"Sure." Nick reached out a quick hand to touch his son's shoulder.

"I'd better go up and change," Kevin said. "Want to make a good impression."

Rae could see the disappointment as McKenzie watched his son depart. "Has that arm been giving him trouble?" he asked.

"Seemingly none at all." She gestured toward a chair, poured a mug of coffee and set it before him.

"You were right. He's weathering the whole thing better than we are. Cream and sugar?" When he shook his head, she poured herself a mug and joined him at the breakfast table. "I thought you'd be back at Pebble Beach. My son said you were playing in the Bing Crosby tournament there."

"Oh, yes, I was. But I dropped out." He shrugged, dismissing the—what was it Greg had said? Hundred thousand dollars?—as if it were nothing.

"I'm sorry you had to drop out," she told him. "But I'm glad you found Kevin not too banged up."

"Right. Anyway, I was planning to—" He broke off as a horn sounded outside and Greg, tumbling like a tornado down the stairs, called, "I'm off, Mom." There was another loud blast, the slam of the front door, a few yells and the sound of a car pulling off.

"Sorry." She smiled. "But the Pascal household on a Saturday, or any day for that matter, is—"

"Mom, I can't find my shorts!" Joey, bare except for his undershorts, bounded in.

"Excuse me, please," she prompted.

"'Scuse me, please," Joey said all in one breath, brushing back a lock of damp blond hair. "The white shorts you told me to put on aren't in my drawer."

"Possibly because they can't walk," Rae answered, sighing. Nick chuckled as she got up and disappeared into an adjoining washroom. He liked a woman with a sense of humor. Attractive, too. He'd been too preoccupied last night to notice. This was going to be a very pleasant afternoon. And maybe he'd have a chance to spend some time with Kevin later on. Maybe they could finally have a relaxed, comfortable talk. No pressure, he reminded himself.

"My brother says you're the greatest golfer in the world!" Nick's attention was claimed by the boy who regarded him with awe as he balanced on one foot and rubbed the other against his leg. "Are you?"

"Not quite. Just trying for it."

"Kevin didn't even tell us."

No, he wouldn't, Nick thought ruefully. "What about you? Are you a golfer?"

"Me?" The awed blue eyes turned incredulous. "I'm just ten years old!"

He was about to say that was a good time to begin when Rae returned and handed Joey a neatly folded pile of clothes. "Didn't I tell you to take these up and put them away?"

"Forgot." The boy scampered away.

"Put on the red T-shirt," she called after him. Then she glanced at the clock. "I'd better get dressed too. Back in a sec." She departed just as Kevin returned from upstairs.

"I'm glad to fill in for you," Nick began, studying his son. He looked as robust as ever. "But are you sure you want to take on a job? Everything's still so new for you and right now, with a broken arm..."

"This is nothing. Doesn't bother me at all. And I really don't want to miss this opportunity." He hoped to attend university in the United States, he explained, and Dansby was his first choice because of its veterinary college. Being known there might help him gain admission. "It has a high rating, you know."

"I've heard," Nick said, feeling his spirits lift. If Kevin should remain here during his university years, as well... "Want me to drop you at the college?"

"No. It's not far. I can walk." He hesitated a moment. "Thanks, Dad, for finding the dog. I didn't like to think of him lying there hurt."

"I know."

"And I'm sorry about your tournament. It wasn't necessary for you to come. I mean, just for this." He gestured with the sling.

"But we had to know, didn't we? And you're more important than any golf game." *Whether you know it or not,* McKenzie thought as he watched his son depart. "I'll see you tonight," he called after him. And there would be other times when they'd get together. He'd make sure of it.

As soon as he'd learned that Kevin would be an exchange student in Dansby for the school year, he'd decided to relocate to this area, at least until next summer. He'd practice at the championship courses nearby; there were seven. And for once, he'd have no competition from Father or the farm. No, he thought, with a soft chuckle, only from a whole school of veterinary science.

Still, he told himself as he poured a second cup of coffee, he ought to be glad to have a kid with a consuming and constructive interest, even if it didn't coincide with his own. And he didn't intend to let it develop into the wrangling that had existed between his own father and himself. Of course, reconciliation had finally come, but not until his late twenties. Not until he'd established a life and a career of his own. He didn't want it to be that way with Kevin.

Yes, it had taken Father a long time to come to terms with his son's decision to leave the farm.

But, he admitted now, it had taken *him* an equally long time to learn to see things from his father's point of view. It must have been painful to have his only son tramping around the golf links with his grandfather when he was needed to help save the dying dairy farm. The farm Grandfather had neglected.

Reluctantly, guiltily, unhappily, Nick would abandon the links to work at the farm. He had made a solemn vow that he would never make his own son feel guilty and unhappy. If he preferred animals to golf, so be it.

Nick's mouth twisted into a smile, and he picked up the two coffee mugs to place them in the dishwasher. Neither he nor his father had guessed that golf would bring in far more money than the farm ever did. Or that the very money Nick made at golf would, in fact, save the farm and keep it solvent.

"Why, thank you very much," said Rae who'd just entered the kitchen with Joey in tow. "I can tell you've been well-trained."

"My Scottish heritage. My father was a believer in the work ethic." He turned from the dishwasher and almost gulped. The way those designer jeans hugged her shapely hips...

"I'm afraid this is an imposition," she apologized. "You really don't have to come. I can manage on my own."

"No bother. I'm glad to help," he told her, and meant it. His only purpose had been to follow up on his son. He hadn't expected a bonus in the person of Rae Pascal, with her big hazel eyes, slightly tilted nose and the sleek, almost boyishly cut bronze hair that gave her an enchanting elfin look. Rather like one of the wee people in his mother's fairy tales.

"Shall I trail you in my car?" he asked.

Rae considered his suggestion. "No," she decided. "It might be simpler if you came with us—if you can stand it. I have to pick up a couple of boys and stop by the bakery."

During the ride to the course, he listened in amused silence to the bickering among the three boys—who got the window seats and who'd chosen the present. This was a new experience for him. He and Jan had divorced when Kevin was just a baby. During the summer months when he had custody, Kevin always stayed with his parents at the farm while he made the golf circuit. And now that Kevin was old enough to join him on the tour, he preferred the farm. He sighed. Funny how preferences seemed to skip a generation, at least in his family.

"Sorry you volunteered?" she asked, glancing at him and tilting her head significantly toward the racket in the back.

"Oh, no. It's just—I had something else on my mind. I think I'll survive."

Although he wondered about that when they reached Goosey Gander's. Within ten minutes, a dozen other equally active boys were deposited by their respective parents. Two of the fathers and at least one mother recognized McKenzie. He smiled and responded rather absently to their compliments. It was difficult to carry on much of a conversation among the boys' shrieks and laughter. Togetherness had reacted like a grenade, and Joey and his pals were exploding all over the place. In desperation McKenzie gave a sharp commanding whistle that stopped most of them in their tracks.

"Okay, guys, over here!" he called, taking hold of a surprised Joey. "Line starts here."

He was not unaware of Rae Pascal's grateful smile as he took charge.

She was impressed that McKenzie's whistle and a firm "Over here, laddies" brought immediate order and respect. She had been envisioning him awkward with the boys and definitely out of place at this tiny fairy-tale golf course. She watched in amazement as he lined the boys up at hole number one, Snow White and the Seven Dwarfs, and instructed each boy on the best procedure.

"Hold the club this way. That's right.... Take your time.... Good shot, laddie.... All right, your turn." Patiently he guided each across the slope lined by carved likenesses of the Seven Dwarfs and around what he called a dogleg into Snow White's cupped hands. As they proceeded along the course, there were more misses than successes, but somehow Nick kept them moving, making way for other converging groups of children and harried adults. He kept the boys' interest and generated a healthy competition. Rae, cheering each boy and happily retrieving scattered balls, was immensely enjoying what she had thought would be a chore. By the fifth hole, Nick had all the boys in the palm of his hand, and Joey had become more than a little arrogant about his new friend.

"Kevin has a fun dad, huh?" he whispered to Rae. "Is he going to stay with us till Kevin gets well, Mom?"

"No, honey," she answered. "He's leaving in the morning."

"I wish he wouldn't," Joey muttered. Rae only smiled, refusing to echo the same thought, even to herself. It couldn't be proximity to this man that evoked the warm sweet sensation simmering within. Just the festive mood and the unusual environment—

birthday doings, with the help of a willing volunteer father. Except that the occasional conspiratorial glances he directed toward her were not at all father-like. Definitely man-to-woman, and the flush staining her cheeks had little to do with the heat from the sun.

The ninth and last hole, Jack and Jill, was rather a difficult one, downhill instead of up. The ball had to go through Jack's water-filled bucket down the trap into Jill's bucket. Only two of the boys had made it, and only after seven or eight tries. Now it was Todd's turn, and Rae held her breath. The poor kid hadn't parred a single hole and the boys were giving him a hard time. He hung back, and Rae couldn't blame him. He was a chubby boy, rather awkward at sports and often the butt of jokes from the others.

"Come on, laddie, have a go," Nick urged, bending toward him. "Nothing ventured, nothing gained. Now, position yourself here, keep your eye on the ball..." Again Rae marveled at his gentle encouragement, his patient coaching.

As Todd listened, the scared, tense expression faded from his face and he seemed to relax. He gripped his club with a new confidence and tapped his ball with the exact firmness needed to send it through the water pail, down the rail to the dry pail, and hole out in one. The shot of the day. Astonishment held all silent for a moment. Then the congratulatory yells began. Todd had made the only hole in one. Rae grinned as the chubby boy's chest lifted triumphantly and his eyes gleamed with cocky pride.

Her heart swelled. "Thank you," she managed to whisper to McKenzie as they moved their gang toward the refreshment table. "Todd needed that."

"I know," he said. "I'm glad he made it."

But it was you, she thought. And not only Todd, but every boy at the party had been touched and influenced by Nick McKenzie. He had become the undisputed star of the occasion. She watched his tall figure moving with an athlete's easy grace as he jostled with the boys, heard his hearty laugh as he joked with them. You'd think he was really enjoying this, that he'd rather be here than on a real golf course, making a hundred thousand dollars.

By the time they reached home, her heart was swelling with more than gratitude. She looked up at his face and decided she'd been wrong. He *was* handsome. She liked the casual unruliness of the thick black hair, the quiet joy that seemed to lurk behind the deep blue eyes, the full lips that always curved just on the edge of a smile. She had an almost irresistible urge to kiss those lips, to feel . . . She took a deep breath and a firm grip on her emotions.

"Come in," she invited. "Kevin should be home by now."

Kevin greeted her with an enthusiastic shout. "I got the job, Mom! Uh, hi, Dad."

"Great," she answered. "Come and tell us about it."

"Hey, Kev, wanna see all the neat things I got?" Joey called over the mound of packages in his arms. "Wanna play this new computer game?"

"Okay, Kevin, would you help Joey first? Take these from your dad and get all this loot upstairs. No games now, Joey. Kevin wants to talk with his dad," she added as she led Nick into the family room. She had seen the surprised quirk of his eyebrow at Kevin's "Mom" and she welcomed the opportunity to explain. "'Mrs. Pascal' seemed much too formal for a temporary housemother. And his innate politeness

seemed to rebel at calling me simply 'Rae.' So we settled on 'Mom.' I hope you don't mind."

"Of course not. Why should I?" he said, and smiled
that wonderful all's-right-with-the-world smile.

Kevin came down to tell them he didn't get the feeding and pen-cleaning job on account of his arm. But he
was to relieve a receptionist for two hours after school
twice a week. He seemed satisfied; after all he'd still
have contact with the animals. And both Rae and Nick
were relieved that he had a desk job. Rae invited Nick
to stay for dinner and went off to do her grocery shopping, leaving father and son alone.

When she returned two hours later he was still there.
He and the three boys were engrossed watching the
progress of the Pebble Beach tournament on television. Greg, who unloaded the groceries, told her,
"Jasper Henley's in the lead. Nick says he's a comer
and he's only twenty-three years old. Are Granddad's
clubs still in the attic, Mom? Nick says anybody can get
in if you make the cut."

Whatever that means, Rae thought as she sorted and
put away the groceries. Greg needed to take on another sport like he needed a hole in the head. Still, if
that would eliminate football... Dreamer! Not as long
as he was being hailed as Elm High's best receiver.

The big family room was one step down from the
kitchen, and Rae found a certain contentment in listening to the sports chatter as she worked. Unwilling to
interrupt their pleasure, she set out taco fixings on the
big round coffee table—freshly shredded lettuce and
cheese, the hamburger in her special taco sauce, to-
matoes, chips and condiments. They all fixed their own
and Rae joined them, sitting on the floor eating her

taco and listening to their discussion. It was amazing how quickly Nick, as her boys had begun to call him, had established a camaraderie with Greg and Joey.

But not with Kevin. She suddenly realized he was taking almost no part in the conversation. Strange that he should be estranged from this father who was at home with everyone else. This utterly charming man, who was so comfortable to be with, so affable, who established an immediate rapport with perfect strangers. Like Tom, her husband. Suddenly she paused, her taco halfway to her mouth, and stole a look at Nick. He was laughing at something Greg had said and was pointing to the screen, explaining the player's stroke. Greg and Joey hung on his words.

As she had hung on Tom's. She'd met him during her first year of university and had adored him immediately. He'd been so charming, so affable, so...loving. Hell or high water, much less her parents, could not have stopped the marriage when the impeccable Mr. Right had condescended to ask her. She'd been so utterly besotted that it had taken her years to realize Tom was an ambitious egotist who only exerted his charm when it pleased him to do so. When it would enhance his own image or further his ambitions. It certainly could not be wasted on mere family.

She stirred uncomfortably, haunted as always by misgivings. Easy to shift the blame for the failed marriage onto the one who couldn't defend himself. Okay, so she hadn't been the best of wives. If she had, would he have been ready to leave her? Good heavens, why was she thinking of that now? Tom had been dead for nine years and surely the pain should be buried with him.

Anyway, it was unfair to compare Nick McKenzie with Tom. But why was his own son sitting there so distant, so aloof?

CHAPTER THREE

AT TEN O'CLOCK Monday morning, the meeting had been going on for an hour. It was chaired by Leon Waters, Corporate Vice President of Coastal Banks, who was in charge of the Peabody takeover. He'd flown up from headquarters in Los Angeles to discuss sites in the Northern Area—which Peabody banks were to be maintained, which absorbed or closed. The plush conference room of Coastal Banks' Northern Regional Office in Sacramento was dominated by a large polished oak table at which each departmental director was seated. And, as corporate protocol dictated, each director's deputy was seated immediately to his rear in easy earshot for details that might be requested by the Chair. As the relative merits of each branch were considered, Rae, seated behind Harrison Bowers, listened attentively, one flawlessly polished nail traveling to the relevant red dot on her map. Mentally she filed its proximity and compared its income to an established Coastal bank as her left hand pressed against her temple, willing away the approaching tension headache.

The tension had nothing to do with the discussion underway, for she knew these banks like the back of her hand. Before her appointment to Deputy Director only a month before, she'd been in charge of the lending program for the region. It had been imperative for her to know the loan income potential of each Coastal bank, and have some knowledge of the then-competing Peabody banks. These recommendations, she thought a little wryly, were probably based on reports submitted by her.

No, the tension that tightened her neck muscles and made her head ache were from another source entirely. Greg. It had taken her a screaming half hour to get Greg out of bed and he had missed his breakfast and probably been late to school. It was her car-pool day, and one of Helen's twins had left his lunch and his gym clothes. She'd had to return for them before dropping the three boys off at their school, almost making herself late. To top it all off, she'd just received a call from Greg's counselor, this time about biology. Greg was lazy, and she'd been foolish to think that another boy's study habits would rub off on him. She had just taken on another problem with Kevin. No, that wasn't true. Kevin was no trouble and the boys got along beautifully. But what on earth would motivate Greg? Maybe she should take him off the football team but she knew that would devastate him.

"I don't understand this at all." The suddenly sharp voice of Mr. Waters cut into her thoughts. "I see that you've recommended this branch in Lodi's east end should be closed. The facilities are spacious, and there's no Coastal bank anywhere near the area." Waters's voice clicked with the regularity of a metronome as he fired rapid questions about the advisability of this move. The questions were not directed to her but to the Regional Director, Harrison Bowers, who floundered helplessly under the onslaught.

"A deteriorating area," she whispered.

He turned to her and there followed a brief consultation about the shift in town planning, the cut-through of the freeway and several other factors, which he promptly related to the Corporate Vice President.

Waters gave her a speculative glance before moving on. But as the discussion proceeded, the volley of questions concerning recommendations increased and Bowers was forced to turn to Rae time and again. She fed him precise, pertinent information, feeling a smug satisfaction as she did so.

Show-off! she scolded herself, stifling a chuckle. By now she should have forgiven Bowers for his remark when she'd been introduced as his deputy. "This job will require more than window dressing, Ms. Pascal!" But it still burned. She gave the tie of her silk shirt an imperceptible tug, wishing she could wrap it around his neck. Why should he assume just because she tried to look her best that she—

Again an explosion from Waters jerked her from her distraction. "Truly a foolhardy proposal, Mr. Bowers! Two Coastal banks within three blocks of each other? Considering the maintenance, not to mention duplicate personnel..." This time when Bowers turned to her, Waters thrust out his hand in a dismissive gesture. "Look! Why do we have to go through this nonsense? You, Ms., Ms....?" he questioned, pointing a finger at her.

"Pascal," she replied.

"Well, Ms. Pascal, since you seem to be aware of the facts involved, pull your chair to the table and tell us how and why these recommendations make good sense and a profit for Coastal."

Rae swallowed in some consternation. She had wanted to prove herself to Bowers, but it had never been her intention to make him appear incompetent.

"Mr. Bowers and I discussed this at some length," she lied, hoping to repair the damage. "And we thought it best to keep both facilities open, at least temporarily. Both have a substantial steady income, due largely to a number of regular long-standing customers who might not readily adjust to change." She went on to give other reasons that seemed to satisfy him. Waters continued to address his questions to her, but Rae was careful to include Bowers either by consultation or reference so that responses were rendered more or less as a team.

As soon as they disbanded for lunch, Rae left. She found her secretary, Cora Steele, going over some data with Ruth Cook, Bowers's secretary.

"How'd it go?" Cora looked up over her horn-rimmed glasses.

"Grueling," Rae answered. "And I don't think it's going to get any better."

"Oh, dear," Ruth said, "Harrison was already in a tizzy. I'd better—Oh, are you looking for me? I was just about to—"

"No, for Rae," Harrison Bowers interrupted. "Would you like to join us for lunch?" he asked as Rae turned to him.

"Thanks, but no," she replied. She knew she hadn't been included in the reservations that had been made, principally for the bigwigs from L.A., but she wasn't rankled by the last-minute invitation. "I've got some catching up to do and I'll just have a sandwich at my desk."

"All right, suit yourself," he said rather reluctantly. "And thank you, Rae," he added as he went out. "I owe you one."

The swift glance Ruth shot toward Rae was sharp and venomous. "Up to your old tricks, huh? Already making points with the new guy on board!"

"Just doing my job."

"I'll bet. I wondered why you wore that flashy blouse today," Ruth chided as she flounced out.

"Darn it! I like bright colors," said Rae, touching the turquoise silk. "And that dress she's wearing may be black, but it's a darn sight more seductive than my blouse!"

"Right. Just like she intends it to be," Cora confirmed, laughing. "Here are the branch reports you wanted."

Rae took the reports and grinned. She didn't care what they said. She knew that it was her accomplishment with the lending program, the bank's main source of income, that had endeared her to Roscoe Cowan, her old boss, and gained her the position as his assistant. And propelled him to the head office. Which had landed Bowers in his place, she thought ruefully. Even so—and she wouldn't admit this to anyone—the rumors that she'd used her looks to get to the top, even Bowers's snide "window dressing" remark were music to her ears. Balm to the wounds inflicted by her late husband. *Don't tell me you're going to wear that old thing? Can't you look like anything but a frumpy housewife?* Dear Lord, she had tried. But Joey's colic and the miscarriage... Anyway, whatever extra money they'd had went to Tom's expensive "business wardrobe" and his country club membership "for business contacts."

There you go again! Blaming failure on the long-departed. When she needed to concentrate on the present.

"I'm going over these reports, Cora. Are you going down to the deli?"

Cora nodded but her mind was obviously on the previous conversation. "Not only did you snatch the prize job from her greedy little hands, but now you've caught the eye of the new boss, the plum she's picked out for herself!"

"Oh, Cora!" Rae exclaimed in some exasperation. "What caught Bowers's eye is my familiarity with the charts and figures that hold this business together. And Ruth is welcome to her plum. Let me make it perfectly clear that I am only interested in Bowers as Director—not in the man himself!"

"Don't knock it, darling! I think the barracuda—Ruthie—has a point. This one's worth going for. Young, handsome and...single! And, according to Ruth, he's tied to a pile of old money. She's after him tooth and nail. But I'm in your corner, Rae. You're much better-looking and you've got class. That sultry blonde wouldn't have a chance if you'd turn on a little blatant sex appeal and out-cajole, out-entice, out—"

Rae chuckled. "Not interested, Cora. Besides, I don't operate that way." *Even if the rest of the office doesn't know it.*

"All I'm saying is that them that has it should flaunt it!" proclaimed Cora, who didn't seem to mind at all that she was quite plain.

And so much fun that nobody else cared, thought Rae as she gave her an answering smile. "Look, I've got work to do. Will you pick up a sandwich at the deli for me?"

"That's the trouble with you female executives! You get a little power and you go chauvinistic!" Cora's imitation of Ruth was wickedly accurate. "I'm an executive assistant and I'm not here to fetch and carry for *you* like a—"

"Ham and cheese," Rae broke in, laughing as she disappeared into her own office.

"Hey," Cora called after her. "That message on your desk. A long-distance call from a Nick McKenzie. Is that by any chance the famous golf pro?"

"The same. He's Kevin's father."

An astonished Cora poked her head in the door. "And you never said one word! When? What? How?"

"Cora, I have to go over these reports. I'll tell you about it later. Just get me a sandwich so I'll have the strength to get through the next session."

"Say please!"

"*Please,* Ms. Executive Assistant! And a tomato juice—please."

THE MESSAGE INDICATED he'd call again later. It was five-thirty when he did so, just as she was preparing to leave. Cora had gone and she answered the phone herself.

"Mrs. Pascal?" She recognized the husky lilting voice immediately.

"Yes, Mr. McKenzie. Sorry I missed your call. I was—"

"I know. Busy. And I'm calling to intrude upon more of your time."

"Oh?"

"Could you possibly have dinner with me tomorrow evening?"

"I..." She hesitated. She avoided all dates, all private social encounters with men, and she never went out on weeknights unless it was strictly business. There was Joey's homework, and now that she had to bear down on Greg... "I'm sorry. I don't think I could manage it. The boys—"

"Please. I need to talk with you. About Kevin."

"Oh." That was different. "I see. Then why don't you come to the house? You could have—"

"No. I need to speak privately with you. And I have to leave the next day for South Carolina. Please. It's important."

He sounded so... so anxious. "Well, yes, I suppose I could arrange it."

"Good. Shall I pick you up at your office? Just tell me where and what time."

RAE GLANCED AT HER WATCH. Five-thirty, exactly when she'd told Nick McKenzie to meet her, and it looked as if the meeting would be going on for some time since the V.P. wanted to see the relief map. She'd had it made to scale. The three-dimensional display made decision-making more precise. It was rather costly, but this on-the-scene review would determine if it was worth the expense. So the whole entourage traveled from the conference room to her office. Rae was in front, followed by Bowers, the Vice President and others—seven in all.

McKenzie, not noticing that she was with a crowd, rose as she approached. "Are you ready to—"

She stopped him in mid sentence by nodding acknowledgment with a reddened face. "Mr. McKenzie, please forgive the delay. I'll be detained for a while. Would you mind waiting? I don't think we'll be much longer." She spoke rapidly.

The V.P. and Mr. Bowers, both being avid golfers, recognized Nick McKenzie immediately. Mr. Waters stopped the whole procession.

"You're Nick McKenzie," he said with awe.

"In the flesh," Nick answered. "But I'm off duty. I have a date with this lady," he added, smiling and extending his hand. "And you're?"

"Leon Waters," he answered as they shook hands. "I'm with Coastal Banks. And this is Harrison Bowers, Regional Director, Northern California Area. I see you already know Ms. Pascal, and let me add we won't be much longer."

There were more handshakes with the other officers and then they passed into Rae's office.

Nick sat down and was entertained by Cora who obtained an autograph. It was six-ten when the group left, all but Waters and Bowers. At six-fifteen, Rae and the two chief officers emerged. The men chatted amicably with McKenzie before wishing them well and departing.

Rae, about to collect her things, glanced in surprise at Cora who was still seated at her desk. "Still here, Cora? You didn't have to wait for me."

"Not you. Frank," Cora replied, referring to her boyfriend. "My car's in the shop and he's picking me up when he's finished work. Anyway, I wouldn't have missed the time with this gorgeous man !" She grinned impishly at McKenzie.

"Thanks," he said, smiling. "The feeling is mutual."

"Oh, how sweet!" Cora cooed. "And thank you. Just wait till I inform a certain executive assistant that I spent almost an hour with Mr. Golf himself!" She winked at Rae. "Hey, would you like me to take your car home? Frank can follow me and I'll pick up Joey if you want."

"Oh, Cora, would you?"

"No problem."

So, after a hurried phone call to Greg, reminding him of his baby-sitting duties, spaghetti in the fridge, and to please hit the books, Rae found herself alone with McKenzie as the elevator descended.

"I'm impressed," he said.

She glanced up, surprised. "Impressed?"

He nodded. "Very. Of course I got an inkling when I was ushered through a receptionist and two secretaries to get to you, but when you walked in followed by all that power—"

"Oh, nonsense," Rae said. "You're making fun of me."

"Like hell I am." They left the elevator and made their way through the lobby. "Just facing the facts. I must admit I'm a little disappointed, though."

"Oh?" She gave him a sharp look. "You've got a problem with women having successful careers?"

"No, no. But I'd like it better if you weren't *quite* so...independent. So in charge."

"Oh?" She stopped and stared up at him while he opened the car door. "Why? What do you mean?"

He looked down at her and she tried to read the message in those dark eyes. Serious, teasing or blatantly flirtatious?

He frowned. "I'm explaining this badly. What I mean is that you seem completely self-sufficient. You're successful, you have authority—you don't *need* anyone's help. And," he added simply, "I was hoping to be needed."

CHAPTER FOUR

Oh, hell, thought Nick as he drove out of the parking lot. He'd said it all wrong, and now he'd frightened her. Or offended her. That was the last thing he'd intended.

He wasn't usually so clumsy with women. He *liked* women, and most of those he encountered seemed to return the compliment, even fawning over him since he'd been in the limelight. He had developed a light-hearted easygoing—all right, damn it—flirtatious banter that pleased and flattered but left room for an easy retreat. He had avoided any serious entanglement since his divorce, but if he found the woman appealing, the inclination mutual . . .

Okay, he found Rae Pascal very appealing. But the inclination . . . ? He glanced at the woman beside him. She was sitting erect, her lips stiff and disapproving.

What had he said? *"I was hoping to be needed."* The funny thing was that he meant everything he'd said. But not the way she'd obviously taken it. At least not altogether, he admitted with ironic honesty. Anyway he should have added, "because I want to be part of my son's life."

As he maneuvered the car through the evening traffic, Nick wondered how to phrase what he wanted to say.

"I made reservations at Rondo's," he told her. "The guys at the golf club said it was midway between your Sacramento office and Dansby and pretty quiet during the week. All right with you?"

"Fine," she replied without enthusiasm.

Another quick glance. She wasn't only offended, she was exhausted. He could see it in her face. Yet despite that exhaustion, she still sat there tense and erect, head high, ready to do battle. Her wariness was about more than just her reaction to his ill-judged comments; he was sure of it. What the devil did they talk about in those high-level sessions? And didn't she know how to let go? For a moment his own problem was discarded in concern for her. She was too serious by far. Probably never went out just to relax and have fun.

Don't kid yourself. A woman like that probably didn't lack for men only too willing and eager to take her out. Or was there someone special? What the hell did he know? He'd just met her two days ago.

"It's the next turnoff," she indicated. "You'd better shift lanes."

The restaurant was quiet, only half-full, and they were seated immediately. The waiter brought their wine, took their orders, and Nick looked at Rae across the table, still wondering how to approach her. Directly, he decided.

"I was telling the truth when I told you I was disappointed that you're so independent."

"Oh?" Same response as before.

"It makes me feel guilty asking you to help me with *my* problem when there seems to be nothing I can do for you."

"You have a problem?"

He nodded. "Kevin."

She put down her wineglass, looking surprised and somewhat alarmed. Then she reached across the table to touch his hand. "Mr. McKenzie, I assure you—"

"Nick."

"Nick. I assure you that any problem Kevin has is mine, too. While he's with me I feel absolutely responsible for him."

Yes, she would, he thought, watching her. All-out for anything or anyone she took on.

"So whatever it is, please tell me." She wrinkled her brow in puzzled concern. "He appears to be a perfectly healthy, normal, happy boy."

"He is." Nick sighed. "The problem is really mine. One I haven't been able to solve for twelve years."

"Oh?"

"My son hates me." It cut him to the quick to admit it out loud, but he knew it was true.

Even so he was unprepared for the shock that clearly showed in her face. "Don't say that! It can't be true."

"Did he ever mention me before I showed up at the hospital?"

"No, but—"

"For that matter, has he ever spoken of me since?"

Slowly she shook her head, eyes wide and wondering.

"And I suppose you've noticed that he goes out of his way to avoid me when I am around and has little or nothing to say to me."

"Well . . ." Even white teeth clamped down on her lower lip, as if she didn't want to acknowledge the truth of what he said.

He spread his hands. "You see?"

Both sat in silent relief as the waiter served their salads and sprinkled pepper.

She fiddled with her salad, then looked at him. "Isn't hate a pretty strong word?"

"All right. Let's say he barely tolerates me."

"Is there—or," she amended, "does he think he has a reason?"

He smiled, appreciating her tact. "The divorce. He was only four, but I suppose he thinks I walked away from him."

Her look was direct. Accusing? "Did you?"

"No. From the marriage."

"Isn't that the same thing?"

"Not at all. As my grandfather always said, 'An evil marriage is a dying sickness.' When I saw mine couldn't be healed I walked away." And it had nothing to do with Jan's adulterous liaison with Fraser, either.

"I see."

"But I didn't desert my son," he said, stung by her mutinous regard. "My ex-wife, Jan, has been . . . well, uncooperative. She tries to keep my son away from me as much as possible. Not because she cares so much about Kevin but, rather, I think, to get back at me. The divorce was . . . not a harmonious one."

"A bitter fight?"

"Very." A bitterness that lasted even after she finally inveigled Fraser into marrying her. A bitterness she'd passed on to Kevin. The poisonous barbs she dropped into his ear had probably been more damning than his own enforced absence, he thought.

Rae took a sip of wine. "Still, as Kevin's father, you must have some rights. Time to spend with him, I mean."

"Oh, sure. The summer months and some holidays. But that's just the problem. At least it has been."

"Oh?"

"That's when my tour schedule is heaviest. And mostly in the States. So Kevin spends that time with my parents. They have a small dairy farm in Scotland."

"I understand. But—" she hesitated "—surely now that he's older he could accompany you."

"He hates golf." *Or me.* "And he loves the farm. The animals, I think. He often trails along with the local vet and he's very close to my father. Rather like the son Father wished I'd been."

"I take it you didn't like the farm?"

He smiled ruefully. "Let's just say I preferred golf." He sat back as the waiter removed his untouched salad. For a long moment, while their entrées were being served, he was back on the farm, milking or loading hay and at loggerheads with Father. He had bent over backward to keep that from happening with Kevin. Maybe he'd bent too far. If he had forced him to come on the tours would he have grown to love or at least appreciate his game? And would it have been right to deny his own father the grandson he loved, the grandson who was so much like him?

"Strange," she murmured, her fork poised over her salmon.

"What's strange?"

"That a man reared on a dairy farm should develop into an expert golfer."

He laughed. "Not strange at all. Golf originated in Scotland, you know."

"No," she said, surprised. "I didn't know."

"Our place is near the famous St. Andrews links. My grandfather was an avid golfer and I used to go with him from the time I was five. Of course I was slated to be a farmer. But I happened to join the golf team at the agricultural college. In my first year I got picked up by

John Spangler and kissed the college and the farm goodbye.

"Who's John Spangler?"

"He's dead now, unfortunately. He founded Spangler Sporting Equipment, headquartered in London. He originally sponsored me and now his company makes my signature clubs, among other things. It was a good merger." He took a deep breath and sliced into his steak. "The merger with his daughter didn't go as well."

"Your wife?"

He nodded.

She was silent as she broke off a piece of roll and buttered it. Then she looked up at him. "You asked for my help, Mr. McKen . . . Nick. But I don't understand what I can do."

"Can't you see what it means to have my son in the States for a whole year? Not in England with his mother. Not on the farm. But here in the States, near me, where I can keep in close touch."

She nodded.

"And living with a widow who has two sons of her own. Who might need my help in all sorts of ways—to fix the plumbing, mow the lawn . . ." He floundered. "Go to their games, take them to McDonald's . . . give them golf lessons," he added, grinning. "Anything. A kind of substitute father-figure, you know." Even as he said it he wondered if there was already someone who played that role.

"Careful!" She chuckled. "I'm making a list—sink in boy's bathroom is leaking, broken sprinkler head—"

"Anything! If you'll let me be part of your family."

He actually looks excited, she thought. And anxious.

"It sounds like a good bargain. But seriously, how will that help your relationship with Kevin?"

"It would give me a chance. An excuse to be near him. Perhaps all we need is some time together. I relate pretty well to most boys."

"Yes, I can attest to that," she affirmed, thinking of Joey's birthday. She gave him what she hoped was a reassuring smile. "All right. We can give it a try. But how often do you plan to be in Dansby?"

"I'm making my headquarters here. I'm already negotiating for a house at the Del Rio Country Club."

"Oh, my!" She was surprised. And impressed. Residences at the relatively new and choosy club were not easy to come by. But she supposed a famous golf pro would have an edge.

"The greens are great. I can do my practice there And that's another thing. I'll sign the boys up. Swimming, racquetball, tennis—all available."

"It sounds as if I'm getting the better part of this bargain."

"You don't know how much this means to me. Actually, when I saw you tonight I began to feel guilty about saddling you with my problems. You really looked tired."

"I was," she admitted. "I still had a headache that had plagued me all day. But don't feel guilty. I don't know whether to credit this delicious dinner that I didn't cook—" she gestured toward her plate, smiling "—or the wine or just listening to someone else's problems. But I feel much more relaxed. Thank you."

"There must be many demands on you," he said, his expression one of sympathy and real concern. "All that high finance."

"The bank?" She could have laughed. Banking was a breeze compared to raising kids. Her worries about Greg, in particular, were never far from her mind. How did that boy ever expect to get into college? "Oh, we're going through a merger now and things are a bit tense," she explained, shrugging, "but it's no big deal."

"Well, I hope you've got plenty of leaking faucets and broken sprinkler heads," he told her, laughing. "It might help if you had a couple of brats who needed a man's influence instead of, as far as I can see, two perfectly well-balanced, well-behaved boys upon whom I'm about to intrude."

"Oh, I don't know about that." She was really laughing now. "How are you with biology?"

"Well, that depends on—" He abruptly abandoned the flirtatious joke he'd been about to make. Not Rae's style; he already knew that. Suddenly he sat up, beaming at her. "Kevin's very good at biology. Father says he's even assisted the vet with surgery and some calving."

She sniffed. "You don't have to tell *me* how smart Kevin is! I told you that's why I took him as a foreign exchange student in the first place. But you told me yourself that oil and water don't mix, and you were right!"

He grinned. "No boys' study sessions?"

"No study sessions at all if Greg can wriggle out of it. This morning his counselor called me about poor marks in biology and I might get a call about another subject tomorrow." She frowned. "It's embarrassing.

Every time I go in to see her I want to take one of Joey's report cards. It's full of A's and B's and I want to say, 'See, I'm not a bad mother. It's not my fault that—''' She broke off when she saw that he was convulsed with laughter. And realizing how ridiculous she must sound, she was suddenly laughing too. Still... "It's not funny," she choked out.

"I know, I know." He reached across the table to take her hand. "But it really isn't your fault. I'm beginning to suspect you're much too hard on yourself, and on Greg too. Maybe he slacks off a little but he seems like a good lad."

"Oh, he is," she agreed. "Never any trouble otherwise. If he'd only give his studies half the attention he gives football. The coach declares he's the best wide receiver he's ever had, but I'm thinking of taking him off the team—if the school doesn't beat me to it."

"Oh, don't do that," he protested in earnest. "He needs the discipline, the physical exercise and he needs something he's good at."

"Maybe you're right. But he also needs a jolt. Something that would make him at least look at his books. He's not dumb. You should see the paper he wrote for his history class."

"Really?"

"In just one afternoon. He had a dentist appointment that morning and he talked me into letting him spend the rest of the day at the university library instead of going back to school. Of course, you know the paper was due the next day and I had to type it that night. But it was good! Really good!" It gave her a lift just thinking about it. "He had a bibliography and he quoted some of the references. But to read, comprehend, and get all that information down in a well-organized, well-written paper..." She threw him an embarrassed glance. "Now I'm bragging!"

"Nothing wrong with that. And you've just given me an idea."

"Oh?"

"Have you ever enlisted Kevin's aid?"

"You mean asked him to tutor Greg? I thought of that, but I didn't—"

"No. Asked him to seek Greg's assistance."

"In what, for Pete's sake?"

"You just said Greg's an excellent writer."

"Are you saying Kevin is not?"

Nick rubbed his chin and winked at her. "As my grandfather said, A wise man can sometimes play the fool."

"Your grandfather must have been full of proverbs."

"He was. And usually hit the target as expertly as he drove a golf ball."

"He was an expert golfer too?"

"Who do you think taught me? But back to Kevin..." He went on to say that a teenage boy sometimes resented being forced to seek help. But if one of his peers asked for help, perhaps in exchange for help in another area, that might be a different matter.

"You mean you'll ask Kevin to do this?" she asked.

"No, you will. You've already established a better relationship with him in two weeks than I have in his whole life," he said ruefully.

"But we're going to change that," she declared with conviction. At that moment she pledged to help him with all her heart.

It was the strangest evening she had ever spent with any man, she thought as he drove her home. All they'd talked about was their boys and their mutual problems. Sharing, not criticizing or even advising. She felt more relaxed than she had in a long time.

"Thank you for a very enjoyable evening," she said as he opened her door and followed her into the dimly lit hallway. The rest of the house was quiet and dark. She hadn't realized it was so late. Yet she felt strangely reluctant to see him leave. "Could I offer you a nightcap?" she asked. "Brandy? Coffee?"

"No, you've had a long day. And from what you tell me, probably a long one tomorrow. And I have a plane to catch." Still he didn't move, but kept staring down at her with those intense searching eyes.

"Oh, that's right," she said, feeling a little awkward. "Another tour? Well, I wish you luck."

"I've had my luck tonight. You've no idea how much our bargain means to me," he said as he removed her purse from her hand and laid it on the side table. "Shall we seal it?"

"Yes, indeed," she answered, smiling as she extended her hand.

He took her hand but only to pull her closer as he bent to touch his lips to hers. It was a light kiss, a brief kiss, but so warm, so tender, that it shook her to the core. She had a foolish impulse to fling her arms around his neck, lean her head against his shoulder and—

"Thank you, Rae Pascal. I'll be in touch. Good night." Gently he brushed a finger along her cheek, then quickly turned and left her.

CHAPTER FIVE

RAE RACED UP THE STAIRS, feeling happy, light-hearted and a little lightheaded. The wine, of course. But it usually made her sleepy and she didn't feel at all sleepy. On the contrary, she felt wide awake, alert and filled with elation. Maybe it wasn't the wine, she thought with a nervous giggle, but the euphoric aftermath of a wonderful date.

Not that she'd many dates to compare it with. But this was certainly an unusual evening. Their conversation had been mostly about their kids. Nick McKenzie wasn't just another guy hitting on her for his fun and personal profit, she thought as she kicked off her shoes. Of course that *had* been her impression in the parking lot, when he came on with that "hoping to be needed" ploy. But it *wasn't* a ploy. He meant it. Because he didn't want anything personal from her.

She took off her blouse and suit, automatically hanging them in the closet. If only the boys would follow her example. No, what Nick McKenzie wanted was to share in the things that really mattered. To him as well as to her. Children and family. He wanted the best for Kevin; he wanted a closer relationship with his son. She did not doubt his sincerity. She had seen his despair when he said "My son hates me." Even before that, she'd sensed the reticence between them. But she had also seen that quick flash of happy surprise when

Kevin saw his father that night in the hospital. And hadn't Nick dropped out of a major tournament at the first sign that his son needed him? Hadn't he searched at midnight for a dog Kevin was worried about? And now he was moving to Dansby just to be near him. Without a doubt, there was constraint between them. But there was love, too. She would do all she could to bring those two together.

She slipped into her gown, thinking that she'd only hinted at her own problem. But somehow the sharing had lightened the load. To have someone nearby who was interested, offering encouragement and suggestions, made her feel . . . well, as if she wasn't alone.

She lay in bed, still wide awake, her mind drifting. Her thoughts weren't on the shared problems they'd discussed, but on the sweet smell of wine mixed with a spicy after-shave. She relived the light touch of his lips on hers and reveled in a newfound feeling of contentment and anticipation, as if something wonderful was about to happen. She hadn't felt that way for a long time. Not since . . .

She sat up in bed, jolted by the thought. Not since that first date with Tom!

Dear Lord, she'd been beside herself. So flattered that this handsome and popular man, a senior at the university law school, had actually asked her out. Even now, she could remember the wild feeling of joyful anticipation. The euphoria had lasted exactly three years. The three years after that, the last three, had been a nightmare as she tried to hang on to a shattered dream.

She lay back in bed trying to remember what Nick McKenzie had said about his own marriage. Something about a sickness that couldn't be healed. But one thing was clear. It had been he who walked away. He'd said so himself. Had he left behind a wife as distraught and unhappy as Rae had been? Had he become rich and famous by then? Spoiled by the glamour and attraction of other women, as Tom had been?

Oh, good heavens, what business was that of hers? Her only concern was his son, in whom he was obviously interested. He hoped to mend their relationship and had asked for her help. That was all! Besides, Nick McKenzie probably had women throwing themselves at him, and she didn't intend to be one of them! It had taken her nine years to build a satisfactory life centering on her boys and her career. She had no intention of messing it up. And a relationship with a man like Nick McKenzie was a dangerous proposition. She knew that through experience, knew the hurt and damage such a man could inflict.

She gave her pillow a couple of punches, turned on her side and tried to sleep.

SHE DID MANAGE TO CATCH Kevin alone the next night while Greg was at football practice. He cheerfully agreed to help sort out the clothes she was taking from the dryer, but when she suggested the biology-literature exchange he gave her his father's lopsided grin. ''No way could I fake it. I'm pulling down an A in literature and Greg knows it.''

''Darn it, Kevin,'' she said, laughing. ''Why do you have to be so perfect in everything?''

''Not everything. I'm having a hard time in algebra,'' he confessed with a sigh. ''And Greg knows that, too.''

''Oh,'' she said a little dubiously. ''The thing is, algebra isn't exactly a snap for Greg. He goes up and down like a yoyo—A this month and F the next." Still, she reflected as she rolled a pair of socks, his marks were all in direct relation to whether or not he opened his textbook. So if prompted to open it... "Listen, Kevin, how about a little quid pro quo?"

"What?" Kevin looked puzzled. "You mean one thing in return for another? But what?"

"You help him in biology and he in turn helps you with algebra. See?"

Kevin gave a doubtful shrug. "Okay, but Greg's not much better than—"

"I know, I know," she agreed. "But I don't think he'll admit that if you ask for his help. Please, Kevin. *Something's* got to make him hit the books."

"All right. I'll...we'll give it a try. And I know I can help in biology. We work in pairs in the biology lab. I'll ask Ms. Morris to pair me with Greg."

"You know something, Kevin," Rae said, smiling as she handed him a pile of undershirts. "I'm glad you came to live with us."

"Me, too," he said sheepishly. "These go in Joey's room?"

"And not on the bed. In the drawer, please."

She was almost afraid to believe it when, two nights later, she heard Kevin and Greg arguing—no, discussing—an equation. Greg's voice was loud and clear. "No, man, this is the way it goes...see?" Greg's competitive spirit was coming through in academics. At last. And a week later a call to his teacher revealed some improvement in biology. She could have hugged Kevin!

She phoned her mother in Oregon. "You were wrong, Mother. Best thing I ever did was take on a foreign exchange student!"

She didn't mention the exchange student's father and she didn't admit, even to herself, that she was waiting for his call.

It came the day he returned from South Carolina and she caught her breath when she heard that lilting voice. "Glad I caught you before you left the office. I thought maybe you and the boys could come over to the club for dinner tonight."

"My goodness," she said, watching Cora watching her. Cora had also recognized his voice and had exchanged a few words before handing over the phone. "You don't waste time, do you?"

"Can't afford to. And I'd like you and the boys to see my place. How about it?"

Mentally she juggled the boys' various activity schedules. "Today seems good. It'll have to be after Joey's soccer, though. What about—I mean, is there a dress code?"

"Just tell them no shorts or sneakers. Their sweaters will be okay."

"Good. We'll meet you at—"

"I'll pick you up. A little before six, okay?"

"Fine." She hung up, not looking at Cora.

But Cora was not to be outdone. "Another date with the handsome Mr. Golf?"

"It's not a date. And it's mostly for the boys. He wants them to see his place."

"His place?" Cora's eyes rolled upward. "What have we here? A permanent residence? A romance in the making?"

"Oh, for Pete's sake, there's nothing permanent or romantic about it. He just wants to be near his son while he's here this year."

"So why, I ask you, is he not calling his son? And it wasn't his son I saw him gaping at the other day when—"

"Oh, will you just shut up?" Rae grabbed her bag and started out. "And would you mind clearing up this mess? I've got to get Joey."

"Sure thing," Cora chortled. "I'm so glad to see you finally going out on honest-to-goodness dates."

"I told you this is not a date. It's just . . . oh, never mind." Rae sighed as she glanced back at a grinning Cora.

"THIS IS QUITE A PLACE," Nick commented as the massive iron gates closed behind them and he drove through the grounds of the Del Rio Country Club. "Besides the golf course, there are several tennis courts, an Olympic-size swimming pool, and racquet-ball and exercise rooms in the clubhouse."

"Is there a basketball court?" asked Greg who was gazing eagerly out the car window.

"Don't know about that. I'll check it out." Nick parked the car and led them toward the restaurant. The dining room was spacious, and an atmosphere of quiet joviality pervaded as the muted voices rose and fell. Many of these people must be club residents, Rae thought. Floor-to-ceiling windows gave a full view of a wide lighted terrace, where a few hearty diners were braving the early fall evening.

"Can we eat out there?" Joey asked, a ripple of amusement sweeping the room as his high voice rose over the clatter of china and silver.

"No," Rae whispered. "I may be a native Californian but I know when to come indoors."

"After dinner I'll take you to see my place," Nick offered, after Rae had convinced Joey there were no hamburgers and their orders had been taken.

"Your place?" asked Kevin, clearly surprised. Except for giving his order to the waiter, those were the first words Kevin had spoken since Nick picked them up. Rae thought briefly of Cora's remark—"so why isn't he calling his son?"

"I've bought a house here," Nick answered. "Great golf course. So I'll be here between tours."

"Oh," Kevin said quietly.

Nick told them he was getting guest cards for the three boys so they'd be free to use the facilities at any time.

"Oh, man!" exclaimed Greg. "Do you play tennis, Nick?"

"Not very well," Nick confessed with a broad smile. "And I'm not about to let you beat me. But how about a few golf lessons?"

"Man, do you mean it?" Greg beamed. "Oh, man!"

"Me too?" Joey asked.

Greg said "Aw, you're too little," and Joey's face fell. But it brightened when Nick said no, he wasn't, that he himself had been younger than Joey when he started playing.

Her boys plied him with questions about the golf lessons and the other facilities throughout the meal. Nick cheerfully answered their questions, unmoved— or at least, Rae thought, pretending to be unmoved— by Kevin's lack of enthusiasm.

Towering oak trees shaded the residential area, which skirted the luscious greens of the golf course. The trees and gravel paths wound past the apartments, duplexes and single houses and gave the place an informal rustic appearance. Rae was surprised when Nick led them to one of the single houses, a large one of two stories. Except for a small powder room and an average-sized kitchen, the first floor was one spacious living and dining room.

"It's lovely," Rae breathed, gazing at the huge stone fireplace and the comfortable, attractive beige and brown furnishings that seemed just right. She wondered how he'd managed to furnish it so quickly.

"It was a model," he put in, as if reading her thoughts. "And I just took the whole package."

"I see," she mused. How nice to be able to do that; it certainly simplified decision making.

"Hey, Mom!" Greg yelled. "Come look. A fireplace in the bedroom! Man!"

"Hey, Mom, isn't this neat?" Joey called, gazing down at her from the upstairs balcony, which overlooked the living room.

"Yes, but don't lean on the balustrade," she cautioned. She looked at Nick. "I'm afraid my boys are taking over."

"Let them. Come on up. I want you to see the rest of the place before I move in and mess it up."

The three bedrooms and two full baths were also beautifully furnished. This was no bachelor's pad, but was clearly meant for a family. Nick had gone to a lot of trouble and expense, she thought, and felt a little sad that the only one of them who remained unimpressed was Kevin.

It was when they were leaving that Joey asked, "When are we going to pick up Rusty?"

"Rusty?" McKenzie repeated.

"The dog. That's what we call him. Because he is rusty, isn't he? Kevin says he's doing great. He sees him when he goes to work but he only took me up one time and Rusty doesn't know me like he does Kevin but he would if he was home. Isn't he well enough now?"

"I think we'd better ask the expert about that," Nick said, looking at Kevin. "What do you think?"

Kevin colored but answered quickly. "He's fine. He can even hop around a little. I had him out on the campus a couple of times."

"See. He's well enough. So can't we bring him home?"

"Well, I...I don't know." Nick shot a glance at Rae. She answered with an accusing you-got-me-into-this shrug. He grinned. "Sure. I've got plenty of room. I'll collect him tomorrow and—"

"No!" Joey cried. "We want him at our house, don't we, Greg? Okay, Mom?"

"Yeah, Mom," Greg put in. "We've been counting on it."

Kevin gave her a pleading look. "Dad is away so much. And Rusty does need a lot of care right now. We...I wouldn't let him be a nuisance."

Rae was half delighted, half chagrined at the way the boys had banded together on this, the way they'd secretly been making plans about the dog's future. No wonder she hadn't been subjected to a deluge of entreaties and requests! But she just smiled and gave in. What kind of mother would she be to deny the boys a dog, even if it was just a mongrel, not the registered purebred Taffy had been?

THE NEXT DAY, Rusty became a part of the Pascal household. Kevin did have the potential to become a veterinarian, Rae decided, as she watched his protective care during the convalescent days. Even the rough-and-tumble Joey managed to be gentle as he painstakingly followed Kevin's instructions. Rusty was not only doctored and fed, but coddled, bathed and brushed daily until his tangled coat was silky smooth and shone like burnished copper. By the time his legs had healed he had captured all of their hearts. *He seems so grateful for any attention,* Rae thought; it made him more loving, more beloved, than the haughty prizewinning Taffy had been.

Someone else became part of the Pascal household. Nick. As agreed, he came around often whenever he was in town. Her boys accepted his presence. "Hey, Nick, you coming to my game tonight?" "Didn't you say hold the club this way?" "Hey, watch this!" They even helped with the chores Rae dutifully assigned him. Maybe it was the way Nick had of involving them— "Hand me that bolt, Joey, and hold the light over here." "Use a crescent wrench, Greg—see how easily that fits?" The boys were learning how to fix things. And loving it! Maybe it was Nick's cheerful, bantering approach. He even got them to do chores she hadn't assigned....

Kevin, however, although he worked alongside them, remained somewhat constrained. Strange, Rae thought, that the boy who had fit so easily into their family would be withdrawn when his father was there. She also noted that Nick was too cautious in his approach to Kevin, never scolding him as he did her boys—"Darn it, Greg, you let your mom's car get in this shape? Get the vacuum cleaner, Joey, and you hook up the hose, Greg!" Rae found herself missing him when he was away, always half listening, half hoping for that little tune he whistled or his hearty "What's going on?" Because, she told herself, he was so good with the boys.

Then came one particular Saturday afternoon in early October. Kevin had gone with Greg to an out-of-town game and Joey was on an overnight camping trip with the Cub Scouts. She was in the front yard with only Rusty for company. Rae was raking leaves into piles, laughing as the dog threw himself into every new mound, alternately gamboling through the leaves and rolling in them. She loved the feel of the gold Indian-summer sun on her back, coupled with the breath of damp earth that tickled her nostrils and hinted of approaching winter. She was busy with her rake when she heard Nick's car in the driveway. She looked up just as he slammed the door and came toward her. "What's going on?" he asked, stopping to pet the joyously barking Rusty who was jumping up to greet him. "Why are you doing this? Where are the boys?"

She told him. "I thought you were in Florida," she added.

"I got back this morning. So everybody's deserted you?"

"Oh, I don't mind. It happens so seldom that I rather enjoy it."

"Well, I'm back now and you don't have to do all this work," he told her, reaching for the rake.

"No, you don't," she said, laughing as she held onto it. "If you must, get your own out of the garage. Raking leaves is my absolute favorite pastime."

"How was it?" she asked when he returned and started raking beside her. "Did you win?"

"Yes. And you don't have to talk. I don't want to intrude upon your solitude."

"What? Oh, don't be silly. Anyway, to be perfectly honest, I suppose I love it because my happiest moments were spent right here raking leaves with someone else," she said dreamily, thinking of the way her father had let her jump onto the finished piles.

He gave her a quick glance. "Your husband?"

"Tom? Good heavens, no! You'd never have caught him with a rake in his hand." Or sunk ankle-deep in leaves that might stain his precious Brooks Brothers pants. As they were now doing to Nick's smart cream-colored slacks, she thought guiltily.

"But I thought— Isn't this where you and your husband lived before he—"

"Tom?" she said again. "No. We'd only been married six years and Tom was just starting out. We could never have afforded this big house. This was my parents' home. Where I grew up."

"I see."

"And where I returned when I couldn't cope alone," she finished, feeling the shame of it. A failure as a wife. And then her floundering after Tom's death.

"Quite properly," Nick put in. "Alone with two small children. What else could you do?"

Little by little, as they worked, he drew it out of her. How she'd returned to college while her mother cared for the boys. Her first job as a bank teller. He laughed as she related the sometimes hilarious hurdles she'd encountered during her career climb in an industry largely dominated by males.

He shook his head. "I take my hat off to you. I can't even balance my own checkbook."

She told him of the blow her father's death had been three years ago. Her mother's remarriage a year ago.

"And now you're on your own," he said. "I think you've coped admirably. You're managing a household, caring for two fine boys, three at the moment, handling a job that would scare the hell out of me, and managing to look like Miss America herself as you do it."

"You do say the nicest things." She smiled. She hadn't mentioned the exercises, the routine visits to the beauty parlor, her determination to be as strikingly glamorous as any woman Tom had ever looked at. "For that, and for all your hard work—" she glanced at all the leaves they had bagged "—I'm going to fix you an especially good dinner."

"No, you're not. I'm taking you out. So go put on your dancing shoes. I'll be back in an hour."

No wonder the boys are crazy about him, Rae thought as she stepped into the shower. *Nick McKenzie has a way of making you feel good about yourself and he's such—such a comfortable person to be around.*

He took her to The Capri, a supper club on the river. The food was delicious and the wine selection good, and again she felt very relaxed and not at all sleepy. They didn't talk about the boys this time. He told her a little bit about Scotland and his life on a dairy farm, describing how the sun baked the land dry in summer and how it was often flooded in winter. The confrontations with his prosaic Scottish father about the feeding of the stock, the milking and the mucking out instead of playing around trying to get a stupid little ball into a damn little hole. He said it was much easier now for his father with the modern barn, the electric milking equipment and adequate helpers. He didn't say that funds from his golf had made the difference. He did say that swinging those bales of hay had probably developed a good arm for golf.

There was a combo that played excellent music, and they danced. She had not danced in so long that she thought she might have forgotten how. But it all came back—the rhumba, the cha-cha and the tango. The full skirt of her red chiffon dress swirled around with the graceful sway of her hips, and her red sandals tapped lightly as she followed Nick's smooth lead.

"You didn't tell me you were a professional dancer, too," she teased.

"No. What I didn't tell you was that my mother's Irish. She loves dancing as much as my father loves work. Is this as much fun as raking leaves?"

"Almost," She laughed.

Again she was reluctant for him to leave when he finally brought her home, and this time he accepted her invitation to have a nightcap. He took off his jacket, loosened his tie, unbuttoned his shirt at the throat. She kicked off her sandals and curled her legs under as she sat on the sofa to sip her cognac.

"I never drink this," she mused, wrinkling her nose and trying to decide if she liked it.

"There seem to be several things you never do," he remarked, stretching his long legs before him. "You're like one of those wee people my mother tells about."

"Oh? How so?"

"Work, work, work."

"They sound very dull."

"Not at all. They're always cheerful at their chores, they love to laugh, and they have magic powers. If you do something to please them they will reward you famously."

She smiled. "Did your mother really tell you that?"

"Over and over again. You wouldn't believe how hard I worked to please them." He sipped his cognac, set the glass on the table and moved closer to her. "Did I please you today, my wee one? Did you have fun?"

She uncurled her legs and appeared to consider the matter. "Let's see. My favorite time of year, my favorite pastime, the wonderful dinner... and the dancing. Yes, I did have fun."

"So did I." Taking her glass and setting it on the table, he bent to kiss her. It was a light kiss, his lips barely touching hers. But it was like a magnet reaching deep within her, drawing her closer and enveloping her in a delicious languor of desire. Involuntarily her arms went around him, and with a gasp of pleasure he captured her mouth in a kiss that made her lose all sense of time and space. For long moments she returned his kisses with a passionate fervor that had been buried so deep and for so long that she was overwhelmed by the rush of feeling, lost to everything but the joy of it. Her fingers tenderly caressed his throat, touched his mouth and slid along his jaw.

So absorbed was she in his tender caresses, in the sheer erotic pleasure, that afterward she could not remember what brought her to her senses. Perhaps it was the shock of electric desire that shot through her when his fingers slipped beneath the thin strap of her low-cut dress to gently tease her nipple. It was then that she sat up and pulled free, scared literally out of her wits. She felt stupid as she backed away. She had wanted this, had led him on. "It's just that I couldn't— I don't...." She couldn't go on.

"I'm sorry. Damn it, Rae, you're a very appealing woman. I'm afraid I got...carried away."

But it was she who had been carried away. She bit her lip, trying to get control of her emotions, grateful that he was taking the blame. "It's just... The boys—I... I don't want to get involved."

"Sure," he said, brushing back a lock of her hair. "I do understand. And I do want to remain in your good graces, so I think I'd better go." He walked over to pick up his jacket, then came back to look down at her. "Thank you for a very happy day, my wee one."

She smiled, but did not speak. A moment later she heard the front door close behind him.

CHAPTER SIX

HOW COULD SHE EVER have considered Nick Mc-
Kenzie comfortable to be around? Dangerous was a
better word. She had carefully avoided anything approaching involvement with a man for nine years, but
all Nick had to do was open his arms and she fell into
them. The personification of a sex-starved widow eagerly seeking gratification. No wonder he'd thought...
She blushed to think how she had lost all control, had
really led him on. And then, feeling like a fool, she had
turned all prim and proper. She had seen astonishment and frustration in his face.

But he'd been a gentleman, she had to give him that.
Exercised more control than *she* could have. If he'd
persisted and she'd agreed—as she'd wanted to—how
would it have ended? In...disappointment? Even now
Tom's words burned. The words he had flung at her
the night she confronted him about—who was it that
time? Lisa Fitzgerald. "I suppose you'd rather I came
home to my frigid little wife. You think I like making
love to a cold fish?" Oh, forget it, she told herself impatiently, maneuvering her car through the heavy
Monday morning traffic. As if she could enter so casually and lightly into intimacy! What she had told
Nick was true. There was no room in her life for that
kind of involvement, and from now on she would distance herself from Nick McKenzie.

How had she allowed him to walk placidly into her life? Of course he had approached her directly, and for a very good cause, she reflected as she drove into the parking lot. At first it had seemed a *lost* cause, but now the relationship between father and son was gradually becoming warmer. Oddly enough it was Rusty, the dog, who'd helped bring it about. Luckily they were in the nearby family room when they'd heard the dog coughing and gasping for air. Nick had reached him first but when Kevin cried, "Let me have him, Dad! Something's caught in his throat," he'd immediately handed him over. And when Kevin quickly and expertly extracted the chicken bone Rusty had stolen from the kitchen garbage pail, Nick had praised him extravagantly. "Don't know what would have happened if you hadn't been here, son."

"Glad to see you took your own advice," she had told Nick later when she caught him alone.

"What advice?" he'd asked.

"Something about a wise man sometimes playing the fool." When he still looked puzzled she'd laughed. "I think it was pretty smart of you to let Kevin take out that bone when you could just as easily have done it yourself."

"Oh, that." She'd been surprised to see him actually blushing.

"Yes, that. Keep up the good work. It was a delight to see him bask in your praise."

"Did he? But he really did a neat job, didn't he?"

"Uh-huh." She'd given him a speculative look. "But he's not perfect, you know."

"Oh, no, of course not."

"And he's not as fragile as you seem to think."

"What do you mean?"

"I mean you shouldn't be afraid to yell at him like you did at Greg the day he left your golf club out in the rain."

"Oh. Well, I suppose it's because I don't want it to be like it was with my father. You see, we were always at odds and—"

"So you bend over backward to prevent it."

"I suppose I do."

"Oh, Nick, why don't you just relax with Kevin the way you do with Greg and Joey? He won't break, and I think it'll make him feel closer to you."

Afterward she'd seen that he was trying to do just that, and she felt it was working. Nick was becoming important in Kevin's life as easily and naturally as he'd become important in her boys' lives—and hers. He had...what was it? Charisma. Yes, he had plenty of that, she thought as she slammed the car door and started to her office.

But he had more than charisma. He had substance. That, and a sense of responsibility that was subtly being transmitted to her boys, along with the games and golf lessons. She liked that. Yes, she was grateful for the companionship and influence he had established with her sons and she was determined to do nothing to disrupt that. In many ways, she felt she was getting the better part of their bargain.

She stepped into the elevator, smiling brightly as she chatted with some of her coworkers, and mentally scanning the work awaiting her.

"Good morning," was Cora's cheerful greeting. "How was your weekend?"

"Great. I love this time of year. Yours?"

"So-so. Frank was out of town. Did you see Mr. Golf?"

Rae, about to enter her own office, turned a mocking face to her secretary. "That's the trouble with secretaries—excuse me, executive assistants—to female bosses. They think it's their prerogative to pry into the personal life of their boss. Now if I were a man—"

"Touchy, touchy, touchy!" Cora laughed. "And all I asked was did you see a certain somebody. Speaking of prying... You should hear the inquisition the barracuda gives her handsome male boss, who, incidentally, seems more concerned with *your* affairs."

"Oh?" Rae asked without interest as she went into her own office.

Cora followed with a stack of correspondence. "He's called twice this morning. You're a bit late, you know. Wanted to know when you were due in and what today's schedule was like." The phone rang and Cora picked it up. "Ms. Pascal's office. Oh, yes, Mr. Bowers, she just got in." She handed the phone to Rae, raising her eyebrows in a what-did-I-tell-you expression, laid the correspondence on the desk and went back to her own office.

"Got an emergency call from Los Angeles this morning," Harrison Bowers was saying. "A question has come up about our assumption of the whole Peabody portfolio. Seems we might be in violation of the antitrust law. They've scheduled a meeting this afternoon. There's a one o'clock flight we could make."

"We?"

"Confession time, Rae. You know more about this stuff than I do. I need you. And you'd better pack for overnight. Likely to meet all day tomorrow, too."

She drove back home to pack, her mind on the boys. She knew Helen would keep Joey. Greg and Kevin were well able to look after themselves, but she didn't like

the idea of leaving them unchaperoned for one, maybe
two nights. Nick? He was in town and might agree to
help.

Nick was delighted.

"Great!" he exclaimed when she called him. "They
can stay at my place. I'll pick them up as soon as they
get home from school. Might as well get Joey, too."

This pattern continued off and on for about three
weeks as the antitrust issue became an exceedingly hot
one. What percentage of Peabody stock could Coastal
Banks absorb without constituting a monopoly? And,
in consideration of this issue, which properties would
be advantageous for the bank to absorb and which
should be sold off? As the meetings about this issue
continued, Rae's detailed knowledge of both sides'
holdings in the Northern Area, their performance and
potential, made her indispensable, not only to Harrison Bowers, but also to the Corporate staff. To tell the
truth, she enjoyed being a principal part of the decision-making process.

"It's rather flattering," she told Cora.

"And it's giving the barracuda the jitters," Cora reported. "Now she's *sure* you're sleeping with her
quarry."

"So be it. I'm not about to let Ruth's filthy mouth
and one-track mind interfere with my job." She wasn't
about to let Harrison Bowers interfere with it either,
she thought. She was well aware that he'd done a complete about-face and his respect for her banking effi-
ciency was only exceeded by the more personal interest
he clearly felt. He always chauffeured her to and from
regional meetings within a day's drive. He would often drop by her house to consult her and made a point
of dining with her at overnight conferences. This didn't

particularly bother her. She had become quite adept at fielding this type of come-on, couched though it might be in businesslike terms. Harrison Bowers was no problem.

Nick McKenzie was. She told herself that she was glad her constant meetings put some space between them. She told herself she was glad he had taken her at her word and backed off, that he no longer sought time alone with her or made any romantic advances. But she could not deny that her heart turned over every time she heard the slam of his car door and his cheerful "What's going on?" Or that an envious longing possessed her when he took the boys off for golf lessons or on some other excursion. Or that she lay awake at night remembering how it felt to be in his arms—that one night.

Perhaps this was what made her so sensitive to Kevin's mood the day she saw him standing at the kitchen window watching Nick, who was in the backyard with Greg and Joey.

Since the boys had been spending more time with Nick at his place, staying overnight whenever she was away, the relationship between him and Kevin had become even more relaxed, even closer. But for some reason Kevin steadily refused to participate in the golf lessons.

But he wants to—desperately, Rae suddenly realized when she glanced up from the cookie dough she was mixing and saw Kevin standing by the window. Saw the yearning in the droop of his shoulders and the stillness with which he watched. She glanced beyond him to see Nick, his hand covering Joey's smaller one as he demonstrated how to gently swing the child-sized club on the putting green they had rigged up.

"Why don't you join them?" she asked, keeping her voice casual. "Your father would be so pleased to—"

"No!" He turned sharply as if he'd been caught in some misdemeanor. "I'm not interested."

"Oh, come on, Kevin. I'll bet you're a natural."

"No, I'm not."

Darn it, she'd said the wrong thing. Of course everybody expected him to be a natural and of course he was ashamed to have people find out he wasn't as good as his father. "Bring that box over here," she said, gesturing toward a container on the table while trying to think of a way to return to the earlier subject.

"Mmm!" Kevin said as she lifted the cookie sheet from the oven and the sweet odor of freshly baked chocolate-chip cookies filled the room. "Can I have one?"

"As many as you like. Wash your hands, then start filling this box, please. Cub Scout treat tonight. Use this spatula to lift them." She began to spoon another batch onto a cookie sheet and tried to speak lightly. "You know, Kevin, nobody's good at everything. Now, you're good with animals...I've watched you handle Rusty, both with his broken legs and that bone in his throat."

"Uh-huh." Kevin munched his second cookie. "Should I put waxed paper between the layers?"

"I don't think so. What I'm trying to say is that a person can enjoy dogs as pets and not be a veterinarian. Your dad's a champion golfer but most people play the game just for fun." She talked along in this vein, but she wasn't sure she'd got her message across by the time the others came in to devour cookies and milk.

Perhaps Nick could convince him that he didn't have to be perfect. Why didn't he urge Kevin a bit, for goodness' sake?

"Because," Nick explained when she cornered him and posed the question, "I am not about to urge my son to follow in my footsteps. My father made my life miserable by trying to make a farmer out of me!"

"Oh!" she groaned. "You wouldn't be asking him to become a professional golfer. Just to have some *fun* with you. I thought you wanted him to get closer!"

"I do. That's why I'm allowing him to do what he wants, not what I want him to do."

She couldn't make him understand, and she dared not even approach the subject with Kevin again. Men were so stubborn!

Meanwhile, Rae had begun to notice that, increasingly, when she answered the phone she would hear a female voice requesting "Could I please speak to Greg?" or "Is Kevin there?" Natural and inevitable, Rae thought, this growing interest in girls. And she was grateful that Greg's interest seemed to cover a wide range and was mainly confined to an inordinate amount of time on the telephone. Kevin's interest, however, was intense and centered on one Trudy Austen, whose family had recently bought a house only a block away. If Kevin wasn't working, he was at her place. Or else Trudy was at the Pascal house. Not that Rae minded. She liked to have the boys' friends under her chaperonage and made it her business to converse with and get to know them.

Trudy was quite talkative and her conversation was most revealing. "It's like Candy doesn't believe anything a person says. Okay, like, there's Nick McKenzie on TV, see, at this golf tournament. And I go, 'That's

Kevin's dad.' And Candy goes, 'Liar!' And I'm, like, I can't stand this, right? And I go, 'Kevin, that's your dad, right?' Okay. But it's like she didn't want to believe Kevin, you know?''

Only two conversations with her let Rae know that while Kevin might have a crush on Trudy, it was the famous Nick McKenzie Trudy had a crush on. She was convinced of this when, for the first time, she heard Kevin ask a favor of his dad. ''Trudy wants to know if you'll let girls join the golf lessons.''

''Who?'' asked Nick, who'd been away on the tour and had not observed the blossoming romance.

''Trudy. She's a...a friend of mine and she wants to know if you'll let—''

''No, indeed he will not!'' Rae answered, sending an eyeball-to-eyeball message to the startled Nick. ''And I'm surprised that you would ask that of your father, Kevin.''

''But,'' Kevin protested, turning to her in surprise, ''he teaches Greg and Joey.''

''Only because of you, Kevin. Because he knows you like being here and Greg and Joey are your friends. And, of course, your dad would do almost anything you asked him. So you have to protect him!''

''Huh?''

''You know how famous your dad is, and how busy. Of course anyone would be tickled pink to have lessons from Nick McKenzie who, incidentally, could charge hundreds of dollars a session for them if he had a mind to go into teaching. Which he doesn't. So it would be imposing for you to try to get free lessons for any Tom, Dick or Susie who happens to be a friend of yours. Really, Kevin, I'm surprised at you!'' A rather crass approach, Rae thought, but anything to get her point across.

"Oh, I'm sorry. I didn't mean... Trudy said she wanted to learn and I—"

"Teach her yourself," Rae put in.

"Me?" Kevin shot a quick glance at Nick, who'd been too taken aback to say anything. "I don't know how to play golf."

"One or two lessons would put you way ahead of Trudy. And that wouldn't take up any more of your dad's time since you could learn along with Greg and Joey."

"Well..." Kevin hesitated, but could not quite disguise his eagerness. "But they've been working at this for weeks...."

"No problem," said Nick, who was beginning to understand. "I'll throw in a few private catch-up lessons."

"Maybe I'm too far behind," Kevin muttered.

"All things have a beginning, son," Nick said quietly. "And as my grandfather used to say, A work begun is half ended." He stood up. "Come on. Why don't you and I run out to the practice tee."

She thought she saw a light in Kevin's eyes as he followed his father out. It was the very first time she had seen father and son go anywhere alone together. She crossed her fingers.

She needn't have worried. It might have been Nick's take-it-easy, nobody's-perfect teaching technique or it might have been the fact that they'd both been waiting for something like this to happen. The strange thing was, Kevin *did* turn out to be a natural. He seemed to have inherited his father's easy grace and, after only a few sessions, was becoming quite an expert. He did give Trudy a couple of lessons, but as Rae had suspected, Trudy's starry gaze was focused on the famous Nick McKenzie rather than his son—or golf. Kevin hardly noticed. His affections had been transferred to Crystal Cummings, a buoyant sixteen-year-old who resided with her parents at the Del Rio Club. She was clearly one of the reasons Kevin elected to stay with his father more often, firmly establishing one of the bedrooms as his own. At any rate, the relationship between Kevin and his father was on a firm footing now, with past misunderstandings resolved, past damage undone.

"You were right," Nick confided to Rae one day when he found her alone in the house. "It was his fear of not measuring up to me that made him avoid golf. Now he knows that it doesn't matter. He can just play and enjoy."

"I'm glad," Rae said. "It's good to see you having fun together."

"It's more than that. He's beginning to like and trust me. Thank you for giving me back my son," he said solemnly. He bent to give her a light kiss that was meant to be a simple thank-you. But her lips clung in a responsive fervor that sent a hot compelling passion through his veins. He pulled her closer, breathing in the fresh tangy sweetness of her perfume, reveling in the pressure of her body, soft and yielding against his. He deepened the kiss, sensing her vulnerability, gratified that her need was as demanding and urgent as his own. No other woman had ever excited him in quite this way. He wanted to make love with her, hear her cry out with the pleasure of it, feel her relax against him in the ecstasy of fulfillment. Savoring the expectancy, he gently caressed her cheek as he lifted his head to look into her wide hazel eyes, now warm with passion. And remembered.

She trusted him. She had welcomed him into her home. She had given him back his son.

Damn, damn, damn! He had made a silent promise. That night she had said, "The boys." She had made it clear that any romantic involvement must be separate from the boys. Quite proper. And he meant to respect that. Nick tried to get control of his emotions, tried to stifle the hunger that was a raw ache inside him as he gently pushed her away.

"I'm afraid I overdid the gratitude bit," he whispered. "See you later," he said, lightly kissing her nose before he tore himself away.

CHAPTER SEVEN

"IT'S AFTER FOUR," Harrison Bowers said as he drove away from the Sacramento Airport and headed toward Dansby. "Wouldn't you like to stop for an early dinner?"

"On a Wednesday evening? Impossible!" Rae answered, her mind already at home. It was drizzling a bit. Would Joey still have soccer practice?

"Oh, come on." Bowers flashed his charming smile. "A quiet dinner, a little wine. It'll do you good. You need to relax after the tough session we've been through."

Relax. That was exactly what she wanted to do. But a "quiet dinner" fencing with Harrison Bowers sounded anything but relaxing. Besides, her head was pounding like crazy. If all went well, this meeting today should be the last one about the monopoly issue. Thank goodness! It was great to be needed, to be valued for her knowledge and skill. But the constant travel, and the intensity of the discussions, her mind jostling all the while with what was going on at home, was taking its toll. And trying to maintain a good relationship with her boss even as she fended him off just added to the stress.

"Thanks for the thought," she said now. "But you know I've got to get back to my boys."

He accepted her usual excuse with his customary good grace and turned the conversation to the dinner she was having Saturday night.

Darn it, why had she told Leon Waters she was acquainted with Alan Johnson, the State Legislative Analyst? Waters had come up with the bright idea that she should arrange an informal meeting. "Have Johnson and his wife over to your house. My wife and I will fly up from Los Angeles. Just for a little discussion over dinner.... That way we'll know if our plans are in accord with the Legislature's thinking."

Not that she minded. Rae was an excellent cook, and small dinner parties were a snap for her. Mrs. Macon, her weekly cleaning lady, would make sure the house was spotless the day before and would also come and serve on Saturday.

"I'll bring the wine," Bowers offered. "Is there anything else you'd like me to do?"

"Oh, no. I can manage." She'd think about Saturday later. Had it been four hours since she'd taken those aspirins? Her head... well, maybe it wouldn't matter if she took just one now. Suddenly, her headache, everything, was forgotten as Bowers stopped in front of her house and she saw three figures, Nick, Greg and Kevin, dancing on her roof. At least they might as well be dancing, she thought—searching frantically for Joey—the way they were stalking around on that steep slippery roof!

Oh, that man! Any minute one of them might slip! Thank God, there was Joey on the ground, with a scampering Rusty at his heels.

"Thank you." She smiled at Bowers as he helped her from the car and retrieved her luggage. Now they'd spotted her.

"Hi, Mom!" Greg called cheerfully from his perch and Kevin waved.

"We're cleaning the gutters," Joey explained as he lugged a heavy bucket across the lawn.

She returned their greetings, but could hardly wait for Bowers to leave so she could coax them from the roof.

Bowers glanced upward as he carried her suitcase to the house. "Isn't that Nick McKenzie, the golf pro I met at the office? He doesn't—I mean, does he live here?" he asked with some consternation.

"No, he does not. His son does. He's with us this year as an exchange student. Nick—Mr. McKenzie is often here to... to see him." *Not that it's your concern*, she thought, her irritation increasing. She couldn't wait for him to leave so she could have a word with Nick. They had no business on that wet roof in this drizzle. And Nick knew it. She could tell from that look on his face!

HE COULDN'T HAVE SPOKEN a word if his life depended on it, so astounded was he by the torrent of feeling that shook him when he saw Bowers emerge from that sleek Jaguar to help Rae with her luggage. He didn't understand why he resented the man. Rae was a professional woman constantly in contact with professional men. And Bowers was her boss, wasn't he? Nick gave his head a shake, knowing he had no right to feel the way he did. But it seemed Bowers was always around and had such a proprietary air. And what was it Joey had said about "Mr. Bowers" just the other night? Something about—

"That it, Dad?" Kevin asked.

"Huh? Oh, sure," he replied, trying to still the tempest inside him as he watched Harrison Bowers return to his car and drive away. What was wrong with him? It felt almost like...jealousy. Hell, no, he'd never been jealous in his life! Not even of Jan, his wife. All he'd felt was a surge of relief when he saw her transfer her conniving attention to Lord John Fraser. And as for Rae Pascal...

"Coming, Nick?"

Startled, he looked down to see Greg waiting for him to descend so the ladder could be put away. Hurriedly he climbed down and helped the boys take things into the garage. Kevin reminded him that he'd promised them pizza. He fished some bills out of his pocket, telling them to put away the tools before going to the pizza parlor. Happily all three boys mounted their bikes and sped off.

The cleaning up process in the garage sink gave Nick ample time to subdue his incomprehensible pain. Entering the back door, he was met by Rae, her arms akimbo.

"Nick, for heaven's sake, whatever possessed you—and I'm sure it was you—to promote that insane stunt on the roof? Not to mention that I've got a handyman who cleans the gutters! A broken arm isn't enough. No, now you're sponsoring broken necks, with yours included. Honestly, of all the dangerous—"

"Oh, shut up, Ms. Boss!" Nick retorted. He'd had enough of this. "I'm not one of your underlings. I know what and how to do what you think you saw. And the boys are not babies. They should do these chores."

"Not on a slippery roof when they could fall and break—"

"They didn't fall, did they?" he said with firm finality. "So you're back from your tête-à-tête with the big boys," he added, trying to muster up a genial conversational tone.

He must not have succeeded, for the look she flashed him was one of scorn.

"Just what does that mean, Mr. McKenzie? You make it sound like a tea party!"

"Well?" The inexplicable fit had returned, and he brushed past her, going through the kitchen to the hall closet to get his jacket.

Rae followed, taking brisk steps, exasperated beyond all reason. A tea party, was it? If she were a man she'd hit him!

"Listen to me, Nick McKenzie!" She grabbed the sleeve of his jacket and he spun around to face her. "So you think sitting through a merger decision that involves two of the most important banks in the state, not to mention the legal complications, is like a tea party! Or maybe a *golf game,* where all you have to worry about is getting a little ball in a little hole! Think again, friend! Do you know what it's like to have the Chairman of the Board and the rest of the Corporate CEOs sitting there, shooting questions at you about how to prevent a court-ordered dumping of a large chunk of Peabody stock—" she took a deep breath "—much of which depends on politics, which *I'm* expected to forecast. They want perfect answers to a dozen other problems for which there *are* no answers, let alone perfect ones."

"So tell them. That's your trouble, you know. You're suffering from superwoman syndrome!"

"What are you talking about?"

"I mean you think *you* have to have all the answers. You have to be the perfect mother, perfect banker, perfect everything. Nobody's that damn perfect. You expect too much of yourself."

She nodded impatiently, having heard only half of what he said, and continued with her own troubles. "Besides, I have to cater to a bunch of chauvinists who think a woman in the banking industry is—"

"Aha, my lady," Nick said, smiling. "Haven't you learned to charm your way out of those tricky situations?"

"And have a whole bunch of them believe I'm willing to jump into bed? And that's another thing you don't have to worry about!"

Nick affected surprise. "Don't tell me you've never heard of groupies. We have them on the golf course, too, you know. I have to practically beat 'em off with my club!" He gave a mock imitation of doing so.

The performance, and the realization that this was absolutely true, gave her such a jolt that she could only watch in shocked silence as he lifted a hand in farewell and went out.

WEDNESDAY'S DRIZZLE turned into a rainstorm on Thursday and intermittent showers on Friday, but Saturday was clear and sunny. The course would be soggy, Nick thought, but he'd better get in some practice. He had just donned his jacket and started out the door when the phone rang. He almost didn't answer. But it might be Elaine, his financial consultant, who always checked with him before buying or selling. He didn't know why. She was ten times smarter about that kind of thing than he was. Or it might be his parents.

Reluctantly he closed the door and returned to pick up the phone.

"Nick, can you come over here?" It was Joey and he sounded scared. "Mom. She's on the floor and she can't get up and I don't know what to do."

"On the floor and can't—Rae." Icy fear twisted inside him. "Joey, where's Greg?" he asked, trying to keep the rising panic out of his voice. His tangled mind recalled even as Joey spoke that Greg had a game.

"...and Kevin went with him and Mom looks so funny and I don't know what to do."

"Sit tight. I'll be right there."

He broke the speed limit as his mind scanned drastic possibilities. Heart attack? No! Rae was too young and vital. A virus? Or maybe she fell and sprained something. When he raced into the kitchen and saw her, he wondered if she could be drunk. She was sitting on the floor, leaning against a cabinet and was laughing or maybe crying, and she kept babbling about things she had to do. Joey was on the floor beside her, sobbing, and Rusty was frantically licking her hand.

"I can't... can't stand up," she wailed.

It was true. When he helped her up, her knees gave way and she clutched at him to keep from falling. He lifted her in his arms and sniffed. Cinnamon...raw apples, not a sign of liquor. Something was dreadfully wrong.

"Rae, who's your doctor?" he asked. She didn't answer. He sat her carefully in a kitchen chair, then picked up the address book by the phone and hastily thumbed through it. He was lucky. The answering service put him through immediately and the calm voice of Rae's doctor was somehow reassuring. Nick tried to keep his own voice as steady as he answered his questions. No, no broken bones, no fever or racing pulse as far as he could tell.

"Coherent?"

"Well, yes," he answered, hesitantly. "Seems upset. Something she has to do." Dinner. He didn't understand that.

"Always too intense," the doctor said. "That's what brings on those migraines. Sometimes... Has she taken any unusual medication?"

Nick appealed to Rae and she pointed to a bottle on the table —a prescription for Cora Steele.

"For headaches," Rae told him. "Very good, Cora said." As far as he could determine from Rae's somewhat groggy state, Cora had given them to her the day before, hoping to ease Rae's migraine. Rae hadn't intended to take any, but today, when her headache became so bad...

"But I only took two," she said, the words slurring. Nick relayed the information.

"Bring her to the hospital immediately," the doctor ordered. "And bring the bottle with the pills. I'll meet you there."

It was the same hospital, the same nightmare he had experienced that first night. Only this time it was Rae inside the examining room while he paced outside. And it was Joey he had to reassure.

"Is Mom going to be okay?" the boy asked anxiously, trying to match his stride.

"Oh, sure," Nick answered, slowing his steps and keeping his voice calm. "She's just a little upset," he said, trying to believe his own words, trying to still the fear. What the hell was in those pills?

"Nick." Joey tugged at his sleeve. "Mom—she couldn't die, could she?"

"No!" The boy's shocked face told him he had shouted and he added quietly, "I tell you it's nothing serious. Something she's taken that didn't...agree with her." But what was taking so long? he wondered, as he paced the floor, holding Joey's hand. "What's so important about dinner?" he asked in an attempt to divert them both. "You boys can have hamburgers."

"Just me. Greg and Kevin are spending the night at Glen's. He's having a party after the game," Joey informed him. "And I'm going to have a hamburger before the company comes."

"Company?" Nick asked, suddenly remembering the two pies ready for baking, apple cores and peels in the sink.

Joey nodded. "And Mom says for me not to disturb them." He looked up. "I get to sleep in Mom's bed and watch TV and if I'm real quiet Mrs. Macon is going to bring me up some dessert."

"Mrs.—who?"

"Mrs. Macon. You know. She cleans your house, too."

"That's right." Rae had recommended her.

"She's coming tonight to help Mom."

"I see." So that was it. A dinner party. He reminded himself that Rae's social life was none of his affair, that he had vowed to stay out of it. But when it got her in such a state that she had migraines and loaded herself with pills— He saw the doctor approaching and was relieved to see him smiling.

"I had to call the pharmacy," the doctor explained. "Why anyone as smart as Rae Pascal would take someone else's medication," he added, shaking his head. "Those pills contain a barbiturate that she's sensitive to. She only took two, thank goodness, but they knocked her out. Best let her sleep it off. Two or three hours and she'll be back to normal." He said it would be safe for her to go home.

Rae, who slept all the way home, roused a bit when he carried her into the house. "Mr. Waters expects...I promised..." she protested as he placed her on the bed. Finally it got through to him that some bank business was at stake. That was the reason for the dinner. And how could she do it now and they'd be here at seven.... She was getting panicky again and looked feverish and couldn't seem to stop talking.

"Look, it's going to be all right," he kept telling her while in his mind he cursed the bank directors. Damn them! As if they didn't have the money to take whatever big shot to whatever hotel! "I'll call Mrs. Macon and we'll work it out. I guarantee the dinner will be ready. You get some sleep so you can be ready and on your feet." He was glad when the potent medication won out, her somewhat incoherent chatter ceased and she slept.

"She's all right now, Nick?" asked Joey, who'd been silently watching.

"Right as rain. We'll just have to be quiet and let her sleep. Why don't you put Rusty out in the backyard," he suggested, handing him the dog who'd been trying to climb up on the bed. Joey tiptoed out with Rusty, and Nick took off Rae's sneakers, found a blanket in the closet and covered her. Then he stood for a moment looking down at her, comforted by her deep regular breathing and the appearance of complete relaxation. "Always too intense," the doctor had said. And Nick thought of the way she'd stormed at him on Wednesday, about the Chairman and CEOs who expected her to come up with perfect answers to a dozen problems that didn't *have* answers. And now she was having this dinner, apparently for some expert who might be able to provide some answers. Again his anger rose at the Board of Directors, who expected too much of one woman.

But, no, he thought suddenly, Rae Pascal expects too much of herself. It would be she who'd decided—or at least agreed—to give this important meeting in the hospitality of her home, to make the dinner herself, even down to home-baked pies. Ms. Perfection. Trying to be a perfect mother, too—constantly protective of her boys.

And who was protecting *her?* She looked like a child, sleeping so peacefully, one hand tucked under her face. He leaned down to brush back a lock of hair and tenderly kiss her cheek.

Why wouldn't she be concerned about whatever was going on at that damn bank? It was her work. Livelihood for herself and her boys. He wondered how much they paid her for all the worry and the extras and the overtime.

He was thoughtful as he tucked the blanket more closely around her. She had accused him of just playing a game. And in a way he was. He'd already won a lot of money and with his investments, he was more than secure. He smiled. Elaine was a clever woman and she was tops when it came to managing his finances. He thoroughly enjoyed golf, and of course he played to win, but if he lost . . . well, it sure wouldn't bring on a migraine.

Rae was in a different position and had a different temperament, he told himself. But his reflections were interrupted by Joey, who was softly calling, "Nick? Are you coming downstairs?"

"Right now, Joey. We've got work to do."

"MRS. PASCAL, YOU'D better wake up. It's time to get dressed."

The voice sounded far away and hardly penetrated. She wished whoever was shaking her would stop.

"You'd better get up, Mrs. Pascal. Your guests will be here soon."

Guests! Good Lord! Dazedly Rae sat up, remembering. She'd just finished making the pies when . . .

Mrs. Macon took her arm. "Here, I'll help you."

"I don't know if I can stand." Apprehensively she swung her feet to the floor and stood. She was dazed but not dizzy and amazingly remained upright. Thank goodness. But . . .

"Dinner. Mrs. Macon, I haven't done a thing."

"It's all under control. Everything's ready. Mr. McKenzie just took the meat off the spit and I've got it in the oven on warm."

"The spit?" Rae felt a little weak and sat back on the bed. "What are you talking about?"

"The roast. Mr. Mac is so funny. He said you were out like a light and when he saw that hunk of meat he was ready to pass out himself. He called me, and my husband told him I was out shopping and would be here at five-thirty. Too late for the meat, you know, so he and Joey got out your old barbecue and that's how he did the roast! Smells wonderful, too. And he's made the best barbecue sauce. I've done the salad and potatoes. Now you can't keep sitting there. It's getting late, Mrs. Pascal."

"Joey?" Rae asked, trying to pull herself together.

"Mr. Mac took him home, to his place. Said he'll bring him back in the morning. That's one bright little boy you have. Lordy! If he hadn't called Mr. McKenzie . . . Oh, yes, he said you weren't to touch those pills again. He didn't want to throw them away but the doctor said you were allergic. I declare, nowadays you sure have to be careful what you take, even if the doctor himself gives it to you. Now, you go ahead, honey, and get into the shower. I'll just go down and see to the veggies.''

The warm shower was restorative and she began to remember what had happened. She'd been so scared sitting on the kitchen floor. So helpless. Alone except for Joey, who looked as scared as she felt and kept on saying, ''What's the matter, Mom? Mom, get up!''

And then Nick was here. Holding her in his arms, making her feel . . . not so alone. And she tried to tell him she couldn't go to sleep, she had too much to do. He'd sounded so calm and reasonable and told her everything was going to be all right.

Everything *was* all right. She barely managed to get downstairs before the guests arrived. But all was in readiness—before-dinner cocktails, hot hors d'oeuvres, the table beautifully set. Dinner was delicious, and just as Mrs. Macon claimed, Nick's barbecue sauce was out of this world. Everyone commented on it.

Best of all, she felt rested and relaxed and was glad she'd held the dinner in her home. It set the tone for a gracious and convivial evening. A very successful evening, for much was accomplished. Both Mrs. Johnson and Mrs. Waters, adept corporate wives, conversed easily while their men talked business. Rae said very little. Knowing that she'd already done the groundwork, she was content to let Bowers and Waters take the lead. Besides, she seemed to have lost all interest in stocks and dividends and which assets should be dumped.

All she wanted to do was think about Nick.

CHAPTER EIGHT

"YOU SAVED THE EVENING," she told him when he brought Joey home the next morning. "I don't know what would have happened if Joey hadn't called you."

"Oh, he would have called someone else," Nick responded, stopping to pet Rusty who jumped up to greet him.

It struck her for the first time. Why *hadn't* Joey phoned Helen or Cora or their next-door neighbor? It had been Nick. As if he was...family. The realization brought a flush to her cheeks, a slight tremor to her voice. "But he called *you*. And you came. Thank you."

"Nonsense. I owe you. You brought me close to my son."

And to mine, she realized, hardly daring to admit how much he had come to mean to her boys. And when this year was over and Kevin was back in England, Nick too would be gone. The thought disturbed her and she felt relieved when Joey, who had run upstairs, bounded back into the living room.

"Mom, can I go over to Johnny's? He's got a new mitt and we want to play catch."

"Not only can you go, but you *may* go," she answered, emphasizing the latter. He hardly heeded as he ran out followed by the dog; she wasn't sure he'd even noticed the correction. Nick had, though.

"So you're back to your old perfectionist ways," he said, grinning at her. "I'm glad to see it."

"Believe me, I'm glad too. You can't imagine what it's like. Or maybe you can," she added. "You were there. It's funny. Cora said these pills work wonders for her. So when I couldn't get rid of this migraine I'd had all week, I..." She shrugged and lifted her hands. "Well, you know."

"Yes. So what did you do with those pills?"

"They've been relegated to the garbage disposal. I thought of saving them for Cora but I couldn't bear the sight of them." Amusement twinkled in her eyes.

"Good." Still, he thought, those pills had done something for her. She'd needed that deep sleep. He hadn't seen her like this in some time. Rested, relaxed, joking. Her eyes were clear and bright and there was a touch of color in her cheeks, though she didn't have on a speck of makeup.

"Come into the kitchen," she invited. "You *may* have a cup of coffee while I think of a way to thank you."

He followed her, watching the graceful sway of her slender hips in those snug-fitting jeans, thinking that if she really wanted to thank him... *Watch it, McKenzie,* he cautioned himself.

"What are friends for?" he declared as he sat at the breakfast nook. "I told you—you don't owe me a thing."

"My dear sir," she began, turning with the coffee pot in her hand. "Clearly you are not aware of the significance of your performance at this house yesterday. I must inform you that a miracle was wrought under the influence of that tender, succulent, rare—but not too rare—beef. Not to mention your special and very tasty barbecue sauce, over which everyone raved. With the special added attraction of a hostess who was on her feet and fairly alert.''

''Do tell,'' he urged, grinning.

''Oh, yes. Alternatives were weighed, compromises made, and agreements reached. Indeed a major precedent was set for financial institutions in the fine art of merging without monopolizing!'' She bowed her head and made a graceful gesture with the coffeepot. ''With all my heart, I thank you. Leon Waters thanks you. The Board of Directors of Coastal thanks you. In fact, the whole banking industry is most appreciative!''

He laughed, loving her in this teasing mood. ''I revel in the gratitude, my dear lady, but I fear you are overestimating what was accomplished at one dinner party at which, to tell the truth, I played no part.''

''Ha! You think not?'' She poured herself a cup of coffee and sat down to face him. ''What do you suppose would have happened if they'd arrived to an uncooked meal, everything in a mess and me on the kitchen floor in the midst of it?''

''Oh, I'm sure Mrs. Macon or someone would have come to your rescue before then. In any case, you and the whole party would have been transported to a restaurant featuring excellent cuisine and fine wines.'' Surely her dapper Mr. Bowers would have saved the situation.

''Maybe,'' she reflected, frowning as she ran a finger along the rim of her cup. ''But seriously, Nick, we did iron out some important matters. And I do think it was easier here than around a conference table or even a hotel or a restaurant, where everything is so...so clattery and public! Nick, I really am grateful.'' She reached over to touch his sleeve. ''It's been hectic, all that travel and those darn meetings. I do think we've finally come to a decision and the meetings are over.''

"Then I'm glad," he said, gently caressing the back of her hand with his thumb. Such a slender, well-manicured hand, so soft, so...so capable. "Listen," he began, "that movie everybody's raving about is at the Tempest. Why don't we—" He paused as the doorbell sounded.

"Now who can that be?" she asked as she went to answer.

Nick had lifted his mug but paused with it halfway to his mouth when she opened the door and he heard the unmistakable masculine voice. Bowers. He'd answered the phone when Nick had called to see about Rae last night. Answered like a genial host. "So how's my favorite lady this morning?" he asked now.

"Oh, fine." Rae's voice. Silence, then, "Oh, what was that for?"

"That, my angel, is for being the best, the brightest, the most charming and efficient deputy a man could have. And, incidentally, the prettiest."

"Nonsense. Come on back and have a cup of coffee." By this time she was back in the kitchen with Harrison Bowers in what seemed to Nick hot pursuit. Bowers looked a bit taken aback to see him there.

"McKenzie, how...nice to see you again."

I don't believe that for a minute, thought Nick as he cordially returned the greeting. The man was obviously enamored of Rae. Did she know it? And what did she think of him? Nick glanced at Rae, who had motioned Bowers to a seat and was pouring another cup of coffee.

"Came over to thank my deputy for the coup she pulled last night," Bowers announced. "A breakthrough in banking history in this state. I couldn't wait till Monday to thank her!''

"This is the man you should thank," Rae said, smiling at Nick. She gave a brief recital of yesterday's events. "So, you see, he saved the day."

"Not really." Nick dismissed the accolade with a shrug. "I suppose you two would like to compare notes on your success. I have to leave—flying out for the Inverness tomorrow."

"I've always wanted to see that tournament," Bowers said, a bit shyly. "Could you possibly get me in?"

"By all means, Mr. Bowers."

"It's Harrison, Nick. I may call you Nick?"

"Of course." He laughed. "I've been called worse." They continued the exchange until Nick had completed the arrangements for a ticket. Then Harrison added, "Maybe both of us. Rae, wouldn't you like to go?"

Rae hadn't been listening closely to the conversation about the tournament, but suddenly became aware of a change in Nick's attitude. A coolness, perhaps. A smile that had grown tight and forced.

"Rae," Bowers repeated, "Nick can get both of us in. Right, Nick?"

All at once Rae was furious, confused, embarrassed. "No, I can't go. I've got far too much to do. I can't get away."

"Oh?" Bowers said. "I can take care of that. You're due some leave—and you need a break."

"I'll accept the break, Mr. Bowers," she replied rather tersely. "But not to go to a golf thing."

"Golf match," Bowers corrected.

"Whatever," was her cool response. "My boys, all three of them, and the dog need me. Particularly since

I've been gone most of the past month. So please leave me out of your plans.''

Nick, meanwhile, watched the exchange with mixed emotions. Was her refusal for his benefit? Or was she really telling the truth about how she felt? Bowers seemed quite comfortable making his suggestion that they go together—as if they did it often. Or was he jumping to conclusions? Probably the latter, he decided and rose to take his leave saying, ''Well, you two make up your minds. I'll have one, two or a dozen tickets sent when it's time. Rae, you can let me know,'' he added, picking up his jacket. ''So long and have fun,'' he called as he went out.

''I GET THE DISTINCT impression that Mr. Harrison Bowers is more than a little interested in you,'' Cora prompted on Monday. ''He can't stop talking about Saturday night.''

''It's the business he's interested in, not me,'' Rae cautioned.

''Maybe,'' Cora murmured. ''But he always seems to want you around. Mr. Cowan didn't find it necessary to take you every time he had a meeting.''

''He didn't need to.'' She was lucky to have been trained by Roscoe Cowan, the former director. ''He knew every aspect of the banking business. Bowers—believe me, Cora, he would have been completely lost at these merger meetings without me.''

Cora sniffed. ''Because he got the job that should have been yours. Now if you were a man—''

''Oh, will you stop it!''

''It's time we women took a stand on issues like—''

"I know. I know. But I'm not taking a stand on that. I told you I didn't want the directorship. It involves too much travel."

"But now you've got the travel anyway—without, I hasten to add, the pay raise and the perks."

"Oh, for Pete's sake, I'm satisfied. And I'm sure the traveling will end now that the merger is settled."

It didn't end. During the next two weeks she had to attend three late-evening meetings and one overnight conference that Harrison Bowers should have been able to handle alone.

"I don't think he needed me this time," she told Cora, who had stayed with the boys the night she was away. Nick had been on tour. "This is getting to be a nuisance."

"An affair in the making, maybe?"

"Oh, will you cut it out! It's nothing like that!" Cora raised an eyebrow and Rae smiled. "Okay. I think he does...well, like me. But he's never offensive or pushy. Just charming and solicitous...." She sighed. "He *has* hinted that he'd like to get something going between us."

"So—why not? He's good-looking, nice, and most important, single."

"But he's not for me. I like him well enough, but there just aren't any sparks. Not like with..." She focused on the report in her hand.

But Cora had noted her hesitation. "Not like with Nick McKenzie?"

"I'm not interested in Nick McKenzie!" Rae said with vigor. "Anyway, Cora, right now there's no room in my life for a man."

Cora shook her head. "Most women would knock themselves out making room for H. Bowers." She shrugged elaborately. "Which is probably why he prefers you—the hard-to-get kind. Our friend, the barracuda, now . . . she's getting pretty nasty since she can't get her teeth into him and his money. She's been telling everyone that his father's influence got him the job. He's supposed to spend a few years getting a taste of the real world—by working for a living."

Rae nodded. "I know he lacks industry experience. I expect that's why he wants me around."

"Apparently in more ways than one. Pity you don't have sense enough to take advantage," Cora mocked as she backed into the outer office.

It wasn't in Rae's nature to "take advantage." Instead, she decided to simply do what needed to be done. She began, subtly and diplomatically, to teach as well as shield Harrison Bowers. One night after a meeting in Chico, he persuaded her to have dinner with him before the long drive back to Dansby. That was the night she discovered that, although ignorant about banking, he was astute in other areas. And that he was aware and appreciative of what she was doing.

"You are a remarkable woman, Rae Pascal," he told her when he faced her in the quiet, elegant dining room. "You've made my tenure at Coastal Banks bearable."

"Oh?" She wondered if it was just the shadowy candlelight that made his handsome face look so serious.

"And I owe you an apology."

"An apology?"

"I said some rather unkind things when I came on board," he said without hesitation. "I want you to know it was because I was scared. Nepotism got me the position, which I was unqualified to handle. When I faced a deputy who obviously knew a great deal more than I did..." He held up a restraining hand. "Wait. Don't yell at me. Let me finish. You do look a lot more glamorous than your average banker."

"Oh, come now," she chided. "After all the trouble I take to look businesslike."

"That's true." He smiled at her. "I think it's just you, so slender and young with such wide-open innocent eyes. And I must confess I heard rumors that your rapid progress might not be...er...attributed to your competence."

She waited until the steward had poured their wine before she spoke. "Well, there's no need to butter me up now. I'm not going to forgive you for condemning me on hearsay."

"But you already did," he answered, not returning her impish grin. "Instantly. And without rancor. The Coastal banks in this region have survived—no, progressed—because you were here and able to take charge when careful, rational leadership was most needed. And for me personally, you've been an excellent, and tactful, tutor. And I'm grateful. I thank you."

"No need for thanks. I was just doing my job."

"No. I repeat, you are a remarkable woman, Rae Pascal. You've done what few people would. You've shielded me without trying to promote yourself."

"Oh, well..." she protested, embarrassed.

"However, I don't think you succeeded in the latter," he said, still serious. "I think they want to take you away from me."

"They?"

"The Corporate Office. You impressed the hell out of Leon Waters. In fact out of the whole Board. And again, I've heard rumors."

"Oh, well," she repeated, surprised and not so sure she was pleased. It was certainly flattering and would mean a promotion. But Los Angeles?

He reached across the table to take her hand. "I don't want to lose you, Rae. And I'm not thinking of just the office."

She withdrew her hand. "Please. Don't say any more. I—"

"No. Hear me out. I know you've been avoiding me. As you've probably had to avoid lots of other men interested in an affair. I want you to know this is not the case. I truly admire you, Rae. Give me a chance. Give yourself a chance to know me better, to—"

"No. Please," she cut in quickly. "I like you, Harrison, but you're the boss. Let's keep it that way. And right now, I'm simply too busy. My boys and my job are all I can handle at the moment."

Again they were both silent as the waiter served their salads. Then Bowers spoke, almost casually, as he played with his salad. "I've often wondered... McKenzie, the golf pro... Oh, hell, Rae, I have no right to ask but I'd like to know. There's no one else?"

"No. No one," she stated emphatically, hiding the hurt that sometimes overwhelmed her. She had hardly seen Nick since he saved her dinner party—and that morning after.

"Then I won't give up," Bowers declared. "But I won't press you, either."

"As long as we understand each other," she answered, smiling at him.

That talk cleared the air; Rae now felt completely comfortable with him. However, the work pressures didn't lessen. The pattern had been set. Harrison

Bowers continued to lean on her and Rae continued to do whatever needed doing. This included not only the travel, but much of his work as well as her own. All the while, she coped with the usual office tensions, punctuated by snide insinuations from the jealous and vindictive Ruth. And at home she coped with the usual hectic routine required by three normal, active, not-quite-perfect boys, with a few crises thrown in. Greg's grades were slipping, again. Joey got into a fistfight at school. And wasn't Kevin spending too much time with Crystal, considering his school work and that job at the veterinary school? She found she was grateful for Nick's lighthearted but surprisingly firm influence and was glad that his attentiveness to the boys never wavered. She told herself that she was just suffering from stress. She told herself that the sad lonely ache she always felt had nothing to do with the fact that Nick hardly noticed her.

She was wrong. Although he was careful to keep his distance, he never failed to notice her. And one Sunday afternoon when he picked the boys up for a scheduled golf session, he decided he didn't like what he saw. He kept thinking about her as he drove to the club and even as he organized the boys at the practice tee. She was getting too thin, there was a strained look on her face and dark smudges beneath those glorious eyes. Of course, she always pushed herself too hard and maybe the relationship with Bowers wasn't going well.

"Keep that left arm straight, Joey," he admonished, thinking that of the three Joey had the most potential. "No, son," he told Kevin, "the course is much too soggy for a game. Keep your eye on the ball, Greg." But even as he directed and joked with them his mind was on Rae.

He didn't like seeing her this way. He liked her cheerful and laughing, pulling the boys into line with one of her quick smart quips. He liked her happily raking leaves, as on that day in early autumn. He liked that graceful, audaciously provocative sway of her hips as they danced, and he liked the feel of her in his arms when just for a moment she had seemed warm and passionate and yielding... Well, he wouldn't think about that. Now there was no sparkle in her eyes, no color to her cheeks and no laughter from those softly curved lips. He didn't like it.

He remembered the way she'd been that morning after the dinner party, when she'd bounced back to her old vivacious self. Then Bowers had shown up and he had decided to leave. He gave his head a little shake as if to clear it.

Okay, so he'd conceded the front nine. But he figured there were still nine holes to go and if Bowers was making a mess of the game... He wouldn't rush her and he'd play any way she wanted, but he was betting he could bring that sparkle back to her eyes.

He found her in the kitchen when they returned. She was setting out dishes for the next morning's breakfast and he smiled as he watched her carefully placing each boy's vitamins in his spoon. Ms. Perfection.

"Always ahead of the game, I see," he quipped.

She looked up as if surprised that he was addressing her. "Oh, it's just...mornings are such a rush, you know."

"I know. It might be a good idea for you to slow down."

She sighed. She rolled her eyes. "Dreamer."

"Sometimes you can make dreams come true," he said. "I was thinking about Thanksgiving."

"Oh, yes." She placed the vitamin bottle in a cabinet. "The boys can hardly wait." He was taking them—and Rusty—to a cabin for the Thanksgiving weekend. Rae planned to spend the time catching up on some new bank policies and drafting a report.

"Why don't you come along?" he suggested, taking the plunge.

She turned, looking even more surprised. "I don't know," she answered hesitantly.

"Why not come? You need a vacation." It would be good for her, he thought. "And instead of just the weekend, why don't I extend the lease on the cabin for the whole week? We could go out for Thanksgiving dinner—no cooking required. Wouldn't you like that?"

Now he was surprised; she seemed not only willing but eager. She would see, she promised, if she could get the time off. It sounded like fun. "But I don't ski," she said, hesitating again.

"Doesn't matter. You can sit and enjoy the fire while we take to the slopes. I think you'll be pleased with the cabin."

SHE LOVED IT. The "cabin," located high in the mountains above Lake Tahoe, was luxurious, with four bedrooms and three baths on the lower level. On the top level, one wall of the spacious living-dining room consisted of floor-to-ceiling windows that opened onto a patio and afforded an excellent view of the lake. The big comfortable chairs and sofas were inviting; Rae spent hours basking in the warmth of fires built in the stone fireplace, absorbed in novels she couldn't find time to read in her everyday life.

It was a relaxing fun-filled week, one of the most delightful Rae had ever spent. And the most restful. When they didn't go out to eat, meals appeared as if by magic, either delivered or prepared by Nick and the boys from the well-stocked kitchen. The boys were all excellent skiers and spent almost every day on the slopes, and at night they all sat around the fire playing Monopoly or one of the other games they found in a cabinet. Rae did take a couple of lessons on the "bunny hill," but she preferred long walks with the dog, soaking in the peace, the quiet, and the fresh mountain air. Sometimes she went by herself and took her camera, capturing the marvelous vista of mountains, lake and snow-laden trees glistening in the sun. Once she even saw a deer and another time, a rabbit almost invisible against the snow.

One day she and Nick helped Joey build a snowman and later Nick took her for a ride on a snowmobile. She knew he liked to ski and appreciated the hours he spent with her. She felt deeply content in his presence. On the second-last day of their visit, they both stayed in the cabin while the boys were out on the slopes.

He returned from depositing the boys and fished out a deck of cards. "Gin rummy?" he suggested.

She liked playing with him. He was a tough but jovial competitor, crowing when he won but confidently nonchalant when he lost.

They played all morning. Then she made sandwiches, he opened a bottle of wine and they ate their lunch seated on the floor before the fire. She was enjoying their lighthearted banter and was sorry when he suddenly picked up a book.

"I mean to finish this before I leave here," he said as he stretched out in a chair.

She cleared away the dishes and curled up on the sofa, sipping the last of her wine and wondering why it never made her sleepy but more keenly alive when she was with Nick. He seemed completely absorbed in his book and she picked up the one she'd been reading. But it lay open on her lap, her eyes not on the page but on him. The firelight flickering against his sun-and-wind-flushed skin made his face more ruggedly handsome, his unruly hair darker. And it revealed the sensuality in the sweep of his lashes, the lines of his mouth. She was consumed by a rush of feeling, so intense and so fiercely erotic that she almost cried out. She longed for him to take her in his arms, to kiss her, to touch her.

He did not.

CHAPTER NINE

SHE RETURNED FROM TAHOE refreshed and rested. But a twinge of the old ache soon returned. Nick. They'd had fun together, been good friends and companions. Would he now become distant again?

When he asked her to go to a movie with him three days later, she was elated. She accepted immediately, although she was tired. It had been an arduous day at the office. Surprisingly, she felt rested after the movie, followed by dessert at the coffee shop adjacent to the theater.

In the next few weeks, he began to invite her for outings apart from the boys—to dinner or a movie or just for a walk. One Friday, after a particularly grueling day at the office, she'd rushed home to make dinner. Nick came in just as she was dishing up the spaghetti.

"Let Greg do that," he suggested. "You come for a walk with me."

She looked at him in astonishment. "It's raining cats and dogs out there."

"So dress for it," he said. "It's fun walking in the rain."

He was right—she did find it fun and refreshing, as they sloshed through the puddles, the rain splashing in their faces. Though she was well-fortified with boots and a slicker, she wasn't exactly dry when they stopped at one of the chain shops for fish and chips.

She shook her head at him. "You do think of the craziest things to do."

"And you're just the person to do them with," he said. She was inordinately pleased by the compliment and more than a little thrilled when he traced one finger possessively along her cheek to wipe away the rain. Although he was spending more time alone with her, he never made any physical advances. She acknowledged that she was the one who had insisted on this, but now she couldn't deny a keen feeling of disappointment.

He asked her to shop with him to select Christmas presents for the boys, and she invited him to have Christmas dinner with them. He accepted eagerly, telling her it would be the first Christmas in a long time that he would spend with his son. Kevin was scheduled to return to London during the holidays, but he changed his plans, electing to remain so he could accompany her sons to Oregon to spend the last week of the holidays with her mother.

One Sunday, as had become her habit, she walked the golf course with Nick while he practiced. They had reached the third hole when it started to rain and they scurried back to his house.

"I'm afraid that's it for today," he declared as he shook out their jackets and started a fire.

"I'm mighty glad to hear you say that," she told him, kneeling before the fire to dry her hair. "I was afraid you might say it was fun to play golf in the rain. There are *some* crazy things I don't do, you know. You'd lose your companion."

The thought shocked him. He didn't want to lose her. Ever. He looked down at her, wet and disheveled. Still witty, still laughing.

"I wouldn't like that," he said seriously, kneeling beside her.

"You wouldn't like what?" she asked, sitting on her heels and shaking back her hair to look up at him.

It was that wide-eyed innocent look and the luscious curve of her parted lips that undid him. Lord knew he'd restrained himself long enough. Like that time in Tahoe when he'd buried himself in a book to keep from dragging her to the nearest bedroom.

"I wouldn't want to lose you," he whispered, pulling her into his arms and capturing her lips in a kiss that enveloped them both in a storm of passion so intense that he almost lost control. He felt her surrender in the way her hands lingered to caress his chest, crept around his neck and tangled in his hair. She was all sweet, warm, wonderful yielding and his mouth stopped moving against hers to ask, "Do you like being my companion?"

"Oh, yes." Her voice was low, throaty and provocative. He caught his breath.

He lifted his mouth from hers to trace tender kisses along her cheek and whisper in her ear, "You like doing crazy things with me?" He felt his heart leap when she nodded, her lips against his throat. "I could think of other fun things to do," he murmured, nibbling her earlobe and slipping his hand beneath her blouse to gently caress her breast. He heard a little gasp of pleasure but was aware of a tremor of apprehension even as she pressed closer to him. The tremor recalled him to his senses. He had promised not to rush, to give her time. Reluctantly he withdrew his hand from the tantalizing softness and still holding her close, he brushed back a damp curl and lightly kissed her on the forehead.

"How would you like another vacation?" he asked.

"But we just had one," she said, starting to sit up.

"Don't run," he urged, tightening his hold. "I like you in my arms. And I'm talking about vacation time. The boys will be in Oregon the whole week after Christmas."

She nodded. Her eyes seemed to question him.

"I had planned to spend that week at a links course in Monterey."

"Links?"

He nodded. "Remember I told you how the links in Scotland differ from the golf courses here?"

"Yes."

"I get spoiled on these smooth courses. So I have to practice on a links now and again to keep in shape."

"I see."

He kissed her on the nose. "I like having my companion trail along when I practice."

"Oh?" Her smile was a little wary.

"Surely there can't be much going on at the bank when everybody else is on holiday. How about it?"

"It . . . it sounds like fun," she said.

"It will be. I promise," he breathed and could not keep the entreaty from his voice as he whispered in her ear, "Shall I book two rooms or one?"

"One," she answered, burying her face against his chest like a small, very shy child.

THE ANSWER TO HIS question—*one room*— had been made without thought, only feeling. A longing to be close to him. A decision made in a momentary flush of passion? But no. The feeling persisted and mounted during the days that followed, as Rae was possessed by wave after wave of expectancy, joy, and hungry longing.

So deep was feeling that when rational thought did inevitably surface, Rae pushed it aside. She wouldn't analyze, wouldn't agonize. Just go with the experience. Wasn't that the way these days? Rae didn't like to think of herself as old-fashioned, but she wasn't exactly one of the free-spirited, free-sex clan of women, either. Certainly not like Ruth, who fell easily into bed with any man who pleased her. Nor even like Cora, who was quite satisfied with her longstanding going-nowhere affair with Frank. "I like it like this," she always insisted. "The making-dinner, washing-dirty-socks routine isn't for me."

It's not like I'm an inexperienced, irresponsible teenager, Rae told herself. *I'm a thirty-four-year-old woman, for goodness' sake. Perfectly capable of making my own decisions, taking charge of my own life... enjoying a simple holiday with a man I like.*

A man I love? She toyed with the thought. Perhaps. Did he love her? Certainly he liked and respected her.

She would ask no questions. Make no demands. Stifling the nudge of apprehension, she gave way to pure feeling.

As she did with everything, Rae prepared for the week she would spend with Nick in Monterey. In the flurry of Christmas shopping she also shopped for herself. Colorful sweaters and slacks. Casual but seductive dresses suitable for dining by candlelight. Dainty, fetching feminine lingerie—and a small supply of newly purchased contraceptives.

They were all to leave the morning after Christmas day, the boys on a plane to Oregon and she and Nick by car to Monterey. Nick spent Christmas day with them, coming for breakfast and the opening of presents. Among the usual gifts for Rae—bubble bath, perfume and handkerchiefs purchased out of the boys' allowances—were two small jeweler's boxes. The first held a short strand of perfectly matched pearls from Nick, and in the smaller was a tiny diamond-studded pendant in the shape of an R. The card read, "With love from Greg, Joey and Kevin."

"The initialed pendant attaches to the pearls," Nick explained, fastening it on, then clasping the pearls around her neck.

"I...oh, it's so beautiful," she breathed. "Thank you, all of you," she said, but she was looking at Nick.

"You should say 'you're welcome,'" Nick amended. "We're trying to thank *you*— for everything."

She was touched. She knew it was Nick's way of thanking her for bringing him closer to Kevin. It was sweet of him to include her boys in the gift. And she was glad he was spending Christmas with them. It made the day complete.

WHILE NICK TOOK THE BOYS to the airport, Rae deposited a reluctant Rusty at the kennel. They managed to get an early start on their drive to Monterey. The weather was crisp, cool and hazy, with occasional shafts of sunlight slicing through the clouds. She was glad the fog lifted so the boys' flight wasn't delayed. It had been difficult to get Joey to leave his new golf bag—a gift from Nick—behind. They'd get in a lot of skiing, though; her mom said the slopes were in perfect shape.

She knew Nick wanted to do quite a bit of practicing on the course in Monterey, so she hoped it wouldn't be a rainy week. She said as much, well aware that she'd been keeping up a stream of lighthearted comments to hide her growing apprehension.

"Oh, I won't mind a little rain," he said. "I don't plan to spend all my time on the links." Something about his smile brought her chatter to a momentary halt.

Nick was, as always, good company. He was so pleasantly relaxed that by the time they arrived at the inn adjacent to the links course, Rae had achieved some measure of composure. It was a charming inn. Gleaming and airy with high-beamed ceilings, heavy, old-fashioned furniture, and a hospitable landlord who showed them up to their room.

"You've got a good view of the ocean from this room," he told her, drawing aside the drapes. "Gets a little chilly at night so you might want to turn up the heat. Or light the fire." He gestured toward the fireplace where logs were already laid.

Rae hardly heard him. She watched Nick's luggage being stored beside hers and felt uneasy.

"You must be hungry," Nick said. "Let's go down and have lunch."

The food was delicious but Rae couldn't enjoy it. She hardly touched her salad and almost choked on her wine as she nervously tried to balance her inner turmoil with the inane sentences issuing from her lips.

"I like this inn, it's so cosy and quaint. I'm glad you chose it. Have you... have you been here before?" *Have you brought another woman to that room upstairs?*

"Nope. The links and the inn were recommendations. So, here's to our first visit." Nick lifted his glass. "May we enjoy it."

"Yes," she said, blushing as their glasses touched. She *would* enjoy it. She was a sophisticated woman! "Don't you think these red-checkered tablecloths make this dining room seem cosy and homelike?"

"Uh-huh." He concentrated on his lunch, apparently not much interested in the decor.

She looked around. "There are quite a few customers for such an out-of-the-way place and so early in the week." She pointed out how the landlord strolled through the dining room, stopping to chat every now and then as if he knew everyone. Did Nick suppose most of them were regular customers?

"Either they are," Nick answered, grinning, "or our estimable innkeeper thinks familiarity breeds regulars."

Rae smiled and nodded. She took a sip of wine and looked down at the tablecloth. She wanted to be witty and humorous but she couldn't think of another thing to say. She was glad when Nick finished his salmon and said he was going to check out the course.

"Want to come along?" he asked.

"Not this afternoon, I think I'll...I'll just rest." She was relieved to see him depart. This would give her time. Time to adjust. To banish the shadows and prepare for the joy.

But when she was alone in the bedroom she was sharing with Nick, the panic that had been building all day burst forth in a flood of dark memories.

"Who wants to make love to a cold sexless wife?" She saw Tom before her, sneering, his face a mask of disappointment. "There must be something wrong with you, Rae—you're frigid. Cold as ice!"

She walked to the window, stared down at the ocean beating against the rocks.

Tom was the only man she had ever known intimately. And she had failed him.

Oh, for heaven's sake, that was more than nine years ago!

But had anything changed?

Nothing but the trappings.

Oh yes, Rae Pascal. You might have remodeled yourself—hair, nails, the works. You might have lost weight and bought new clothes. But what do you know about pleasing a man?

For nine years, she'd told herself she was too busy. But that wasn't the real reason she'd avoided personal contact with any man. It was because she knew what she was—and what she wasn't. Tom . . .

But Nick wasn't Tom. She pressed her face against the windowpane and thought about Nick. So tall and lean, so handsome in that lavender cashmere sweater. No. She shook her head against the windowpane. That was not what she loved about Nick. Not his tall muscular virility, not his dark sensitive eyes or handsome bronzed face. She loved what he was inside. His warmth and caring, his understanding. His light-handed but firm command of the boys—yes, and of herself. His gentleness. Dependability. Laughter.

She loved him. For the first time she truly admitted it and the realization hit her with the force of the oncoming tide. Her heart pounded as fiercely as the waves pounded against the rocks below. She hadn't felt this way since she was eighteen. She loved Nick—with all the fervor she had felt for Tom!

She drew back from the window, her hand pressed to her mouth. No. What she had felt for Tom was an immature infatuation compared to the intensity of love she felt for Nick. Never before had she felt such tenderness, adoration and passionate longing. She wanted to belong to him, to please him. But could she? She had failed her husband in the most meaningful part of the relationship between a man and a woman. Hadn't he told her so over and over again?

She could not bear to fail Nick. Could not bear to have him look at her as Tom had, could not bear for him to know.

She picked up the phone and called for a rental car, then hastily scribbled a note to Nick. "Truly sorry—an emergency. Imperative that I return at once. Will explain later."

CHAPTER TEN

NICK WAS WHISTLING softly as he ran up the stairs. He tapped lightly on the door. No answer. He slipped the key into the lock and let himself in. Quietly, in case she was asleep.

The room was undisturbed, in perfect order. The silence settled around him like a cloud. Where was she? Downstairs? Had she gone for a walk? He set his golf bag down and looked around. Then he saw the note on the bureau and picked it up.

When he read it he frowned. Emergency? Not the boys. She would have told him. Work? He looked at the phone. Well, he sure couldn't call the bank as if he was checking up on her. And she wouldn't have reached home yet unless she'd chartered a flight. He could ask at the desk when and how she'd left, see if there'd been any incoming calls. Well, hell! He wasn't going to.

Not that he gave a damn what the desk clerk thought. What mattered was the deep depression that had gripped him. This all-pervasive sense of loss. As if something far more than a week's vacation had been irrevocably banished from his life. As if Rae Pascal had made a choice.

He stretched across the bed, his hands behind his head, and stared at the ceiling. During the past few weeks he'd had high hopes. They had been so close. He had gambled that this week would bring them closer. But today... He couldn't put a finger on it, but he'd sensed a difference in her. She was holding something back, yet she kept spitting out all those rapid-fire comments on trivia. Not her usual sharp, witty, funny self. Something had been worrying her.

Okay, McKenzie. Face it. You've always known a woman like Rae wouldn't lack for admirers. Also, being Rae, she wouldn't play the field. A private one-man woman, not given to casual vacations with another. Except on an impulse, which she might regret? Or provoked by a spat? And if he called...

Oh, hell! It *could* be bank business or a friend in trouble or any number of things. But then, why wouldn't she tell him, have him drive her back? He thought about it, rationalized, wondered, and under all the speculations loomed the specter of Harrison Bowers.

SHE HADN'T BEEN HOME ten minutes when the phone rang. With a feeling of apprehension she picked it up.

"Hello."

"So you got home all right?" She could hear the relief hovering above the anger. "I've been calling for the past hour."

"I'm sorry, but you needn't have worried. The drive was—"

"Why the hell did you take off like that? I would have driven you back."

And I would have had to explain what I couldn't explain. "I...I didn't want to break into your practice session."

"Nonsense. I would have—anyway, why? What happened?"

"Something . . . I had to be here."

"Oh?"

"At the bank. They needed me right away. I . . . I have to be there in the morning."

"I see." Disbelief.

She stumbled through a tangled ramble of explanations. Some dreadful miscalculation, a mess that would take all week to unravel. She was so sorry it had happened just now.

"I see." He posed no more questions but she could tell he was puzzled. Suspicious. Irate?

"I am . . . really . . . so very sorry." Her voice broke. "I . . . I was looking forward—"

"Oh, well. These things happen. It's too bad." He didn't say "Next time." He didn't say "When I return" or "I'll be in touch." Just that he was glad she'd made it back safely, was sure she could handle the crisis at work, and "Goodbye." The heartrending sound of finality made her want to cry.

But she couldn't cry. The misery was too deep. Banked behind dry eyes, it stuck in her throat and churned inside her. Wearily she opened her bag and began to unpack her clothes. Lovely clothes meant to enhance a wonderful week with a man she loved.

And she had run away. Lost him forever? Perhaps if she called him back . . . But what could she say? *Sorry. I made a mistake. There's no trouble at the bank, after all. I could easily return. . . .* That was stupid. She held the filmy negligee against her cheek and stared at the phone. She could say—

Almost in a daze she saw that the red light was blinking. It must have been blinking all this time and she'd been too preoccupied to notice. Her mother? Or maybe Nick had left a message when he called before. Almost eagerly she flipped the switch.

"Kevin, Mrs. Pascal, this is Jan Fraser." Kevin's mother. She sounded extremely agitated. "I've been trying since Christmas Eve to get through but with the holiday chaos... Now that I have finally made a connection you seem to be unavailable. Please, I would appreciate it if you or Kevin would call immediately upon receiving this message."

Oh, dear. She had reminded Kevin twice that he should call his mother, but they'd all been so busy with Christmas. Well, he had written her about his change of plans and sent presents and if she hadn't been able to get through, he probably wouldn't have, either. That was as good an excuse as any, Rae thought as she picked up the phone and dialed.

She was bombarded by an onslaught of recriminations that completely disarmed her. She couldn't discern whether they were directed at the difficulties of communication during holidays or at the thoughtless son who had failed to inform her of his plans in time to prevent disrupting hers.

"Oh, but he did," Rae insisted. She was sure Kevin had written. Yes, the woman responded, she'd received Kevin's letter but not until they'd returned to London on Christmas Eve. "We were expected to remain in Brussels.... So tiresome, these diplomatic missions." Lady Fraser sighed. "And of course Lord Fraser says I'm absolutely indispensable at the many social functions he's required to host and to attend. But our son comes first, especially at Christmas! So we rushed back only to find that Kevin had changed his plans on some last-minute whim."

She sounded so irate that Rae felt she should explain. "It wasn't exactly a whim. He thought it would be nice to spend this Christmas with his father because—"

"His *father?*" Lady Fraser sounded as if Rae had mentioned someone from outer space. "Are you telling me Kevin has been in contact with *Nick?*"

"Why, yes." Didn't these people communicate with each other? Surely Kevin must have mentioned Nick at least once in the past four months! "He...he sees him quite often."

"Really?" The sound of fingers drumming on a table and Rae thought she heard Jan murmuring, "Might have known." "Mrs. Pascal, do you have Mr. McKenzie's phone number?"

"Oh, yes." She saw no reason not to give it to her. And no reason to tell her where he could be reached at present. No reason, either, why Kevin's vacation should be spoiled, so Rae didn't volunteer where he could be reached in Oregon. Lady Fraser didn't ask. She seemed to have lost all interest in Kevin. She thanked Rae and hastily broke the connection.

It was a miserable week, without the boys, without Nick. With only Rusty, fretful and bored, for company. Rae returned to work since that was the excuse she'd given, but there wasn't much point. Half the staff was off and the other half engulfed in the aftermath of Christmas or busy preparing to celebrate the incoming year. Rae spent New Year's Eve as she did each year, playing bridge with Helen's couples club. Though never interested in the eligible bachelor Helen hopefully paired her with, Rae usually enjoyed the party. This year she didn't. She couldn't seem to concentrate on the game and kept wondering what Nick was doing.

The boys came back, glowing from a week of skiing and "Grandma's cooking" and returned to school. Work at the bank settled into the usual routine. Nick had not returned. He did phone Kevin, who was upset when his father revealed that he would be away for some time.

Rae told herself that she was glad Nick would be away a little longer. It would give her time. Time for what? To read a sex manual? Think of something to say to Nick that would recapture the wonderful relationship that had just begun—and just as abruptly ended? Reconcile herself to the fact that it was gone, finished, over. And it *was* over. Otherwise Nick would have phoned her again.

It was Lady Fraser who called again. "That number you gave me for Nick. I've been calling constantly and he's never there."

"I believe he's out of town," Rae said carefully.

"Then can you tell me where he can be reached?" the woman asked in a sharp voice.

"No, I'm sorry. I have no idea."

"This number you gave me is the same area code as yours. I was under the impression that Nick makes his residence in Florida while he is in the States."

"Oh? I think he decided to stay in this area so he could be near Kevin."

"The nerve of him! I hope he's not interfering!"

"Interfering?"

"With Kevin. I'd not like him to undermine all the values Lord Fraser and I have instilled in our son."

Values? What in the world was she talking about?

"Oh, no," Rae said, rather resenting the "our" that implied Kevin was the exclusive property of Jan and her lord. No wonder Rae had initially had the impression that Kevin's real father was dead. "Kevin's fine. He's a wonderful boy. We enjoy him so much and I think he's benefiting from his stay here."

"Keeping up his grades?"

"Yes, indeed. And he's skiing and playing golf and even has a part-time job at the veterinary college!" Rae enthusiastically reported. The effect was not what she'd expected.

"Golf! And what do you mean by allowing him to take a part-time job? And at a veterinary facility of all places!"

Rae, somewhat taken aback, replied that it was what Kevin wanted, "And since he has his father's approval—"

"His father! What in the world has he to do with anything?"

Speechless, Rae made no reply. Evidently Lady Fraser expected none. She made several half-audible remarks about "What I might have expected" and "Against my better judgment" and "Never mind, I'll take care of it immediately!"

Two days later, on Saturday morning, Lady Jan Fraser arrived in Dansby. She was stunningly beautiful. Her abundant silky black hair was carefully coiffured to enhance the exquisite features in a face as pale and smooth as polished marble. And as cold. She arrived at the house via taxi, unannounced, and for a fraction of a second, her cool dark eyes peered suspiciously around as if in search of a culprit or some misdemeanor that would expose the family. Then her manner immediately became warm and effusive, if a shade patronizing.

"Mrs. Pascal, I presume? How do you do? I am Lady Fraser and I am delighted to greet you in person at last."

"What a pleasant surprise. Kevin will be so pleased," Rae said, acutely conscious of her Saturday housecleaning clothes—an old sweatsuit—and her lack of makeup. She was making her guest welcome when all three boys, an excited Rusty in tow, burst in, rather grubby from a game of basketball at the nearby park.

Kevin looked far more surprised than pleased as he moved forward to kiss his mother's cheek. "Mother! You didn't tell me you were coming."

"There seem to be several things you have not told me," Lady Fraser replied, giving her son a proprietary hug before making a few perfunctory remarks to Greg and Joey. Then she turned to Kevin. "Where is your father?" she demanded as if he was the culprit for whom her eyes had searched. When Kevin replied that he wasn't quite sure but thought he was in Augusta, she gave a derisive shrug. "Such a vagabond!" After another brief exchange of politeness with the family, she told Kevin to make himself presentable and took him off to her hotel for lunch and "a talk."

Rae watched them depart, feeling as if she'd just been visited by a whirlwind. When Kevin returned from the talk with his mother in a rather sullen mood, she didn't question him. But she did wonder if he was as constrained with his mother as he had been with his father. And what on earth had Lady Fraser said to make him so disgruntled? Wanting to extend the proper hospitality, as well as to assure her that Kevin was happy and doing well, Rae phoned Lady Fraser and invited her to dinner with the family the next day.

"That is very kind of you, Mrs. Pascal. But I would prefer that you have dinner here with me. Alone. As a matter of fact, I was about to ring you." She had several important engagements that made it necessary to return to England immediately, she explained, and there were some things they should discuss before she left.

"I want you to know that what I am going to say is no reflection upon you, Mrs. Pascal," Lady Fraser said as soon as they were seated in the hotel dining room. "I can tell that Kevin is happy with you and we could not have entrusted our son to a better guardian. Of course, that is no more than we expected," she added, giving Rae a somewhat smug if apologetic smile. "I must confess that Lord Fraser had you thoroughly investigated before releasing Kevin to your care."

"Oh, dear! I hope you didn't find out about my aunt!" Rae joked.

"Your aunt? What about your aunt?" Lady Fraser asked, dead serious.

"Just kidding," Rae said quickly. She should have known this woman had no sense of humor. "I—I'm glad that I . . . met your standards."

"Yes." Lady Fraser looked a little uncertain. "Well, the thing is, Mrs. Pascal, it is most unfortunate that Nick has turned up."

"Turned up?"

"Out of the blue, so to speak. Lord Fraser and I have tried to keep Kevin away from Nick as much as possible. Nick has no ambition whatsoever."

No ambition? "But he's a champion—"

Lady Fraser waved that aside. "I mean, he has no conception of the proper values. Nick is titled, you know."

"No, I didn't." Rae didn't hide her astonishment.

"Naturally. Nick never mentions it. I wouldn't have known had I not discovered it for myself. Some fool of an ancestor—his great-grandfather—I think, just cast it aside and turned the manor into a . . . a *milk farm*. It was on one of my infrequent visits to the farm that I discovered memorabilia and records of the inheritance. You can imagine my surprise!"

"Yes," Rae murmured. "I can." Just as she could imagine those prying eyes ferreting out any family secret.

"Of course, it's Nick's father who's the baron, but as I tried to tell Nick, the mere mention of even a relatively minor rank would be an entrée into the right circles. But I couldn't convince Nick how important it was to establish the proper social standing—especially when it was rightfully his and would mean so much to Kevin. All Nick thinks of is his golf and his women!"

The "women" stung but Rae ignored it. "Golf is his profession."

Lady Fraser's eyebrows lifted. "A profession? Golf? Simply a means to an end. But once he was financially launched . . ." She shook her head. "The money, the title, and the right connections—oh, he could have gone far. But he refused to see it. And now he's trying to force his bourgeois views onto Kevin, even though he has no interest in his son whatsoever."

"Oh, that's not true! At least, it doesn't seem to be from my four months' experience," Rae declared. "He seems genuinely interested in Kevin. In fact he moved here soon after Kevin's accident primarily to be near him."

"Is that what you think?"

"Yes. In fact he said so."

"My dear, how can you be so naive?" Jan broke in. "Now that I've seen you, I know *you* are the attraction. Not Kevin." Lady Fraser's look was so insinuating that Rae blushed.

"That's not true," she said again, more sharply. With a sardonic smile she slowly added, "I'd say you've damned me with faint praise, Lady Fraser. A diplomatic faux pas?"

The quip had instant effect. Jan nearly choked. Her bone-white face turned crimson and her mouth remained agape for at least five seconds. Then she gave a short laugh. "Touché," she conceded softly. "But, Rae—may I call you Rae?—I really do mean to praise you. But more particularly to warn you, my dear. I know Nick. It's always been this way."

"It? What are you saying?"

"A pretty face, a pleasing figure—and, voilà, a new interest. You've seen, no doubt, how Nick turns on the charm. You can't imagine what I went through from almost the first months of our marriage. Several affairs and a veritable flock of one-nighters."

Rae stared at her. That didn't sound like Nick. "I wouldn't have thought—I mean, I didn't get that impression."

Lady Fraser's pitying expression seemed to repeat her earlier words—"How can you be so naive?" She shook her head. "Once a man is in the limelight, my dear, he has...opportunities. And have no doubt, a man like Nick avails himself of such opportunities." She began to pour out a tale of Nick's neglect of her and Kevin, a tale that reminded Rae so strongly of Tom's behavior during her own marriage that she was shocked into silence. After all, she'd known Nick for only a few months. This woman had been married to him. Tom, too, had turned on his charm for other women. And Rae had to admit that if Nick's intention was to charm her, he'd succeeded. Had she been taken in by him, just as at eighteen she was taken in by the charming, dynamic, deceitful Tom Pascal? She tried to focus on Lady Fraser's conversation, which was now back on Kevin and how she wouldn't tolerate his father's interference.

"So you understand why I'm appealing to you."

"To me?" For what? Rae wondered. She had been too full of doubts and misgivings, too immersed in her own misery, to really listen.

"I don't like Kevin being encouraged to waste time on golf. I have already instructed him to quit this idiotic job. I certainly will not countenance this notion of his to become a . . . an animal doctor. Kevin will be a diplomat like his stepfather. I don't want Nick to interfere and I want you to tell him so!"

Rae stared at her. She wasn't going to tell Nick anything and even if she did . . . "What makes you think Nick would listen to me?"

"Oh, he always listens to the woman who is currently, shall we say, close to him," Lady Fraser said and Rae wondered again if it was meant as a compliment or an insult. She realized she didn't much care. And although she was more confused and fearful than ever about getting involved with Nick, she was sure of one thing. A boy had the right to know his father. And a man had the right to know his son.

CHAPTER ELEVEN

RUMORS WERE RAMPANT that Harrison Bowers was leaving.

Speculation had it that he was to be moved up to the Corporate Office. No, a different source reported, he was being transferred to some minor position in the boondocks. No, still others claimed, he was leaving the bank to take a position with a brokerage firm. And accompanying all these contradictory rumors was frantic speculation about who would assume the directorship of the Northern Region. It would be the Deputy Director of the Southern Region. No, one of the vice presidents from the Corporate Office. Rae Pascal? Nonsense, no one already on staff had ever been appointed to such a high-level job. And no woman had ever been Director of any region. Well, she'd wormed her way up to Deputy Director, hadn't she? Ruth was heard to comment. "She's a conniving bitch who would do anything—and I do mean anything—to get to the top."

"If you do get there," Cora declared, having informed Rae of the other woman's remarks, "I hope you'll see that the barracuda gets her walking papers."

Rae only shrugged. Rumors and snide remarks were all part of the game. She had already spoken to Bowers about promoting Ruth, probably to Loan Officer.

She was innovative, aggressive, capable. Overqualified for her current position. No wonder she was frustrated.

Rae wondered whether Cora would resent Ruth's promotion. Maybe. On the other hand, maybe not. Cora enjoyed being an executive assistant; the job suited her perfectly. And many of her complaints about Ruth were generated by loyalty to Rae.

"Well, they darn well ought to make you Director," Cora declared, "You're doing all the work."

"If you'd been a man you'd have had the position long ago," Cora added, launching a tirade against sexism. Rae only half listened. Her mind was on the rising deficiency rate in loan collections at two of the Chico branches. The economy or poor management? The new manager at that promising San Francisco branch was not generating the amount of new business expected. Should he be transferred? Rae sighed. She must be tired. She'd always found her work challenging and exciting. Now she was suddenly weary of dealing with constantly recurring problems, weary of trying to ferret out the underlying causes. Tired of juggling personnel to create a more efficient operation and keep everybody happy at the same time. Tired of twisting and turning in a complicated work arena.

She thought of Nick—possibly because he was always at the back of her mind. Possibly because she longed to be trailing along a fairway with him, enjoying the sun on her back, breathing in the fresh air. She sighed, a bit enviously, at the thought of playing a game for a living. Being outside, having fun, not worrying about office politics or work pressures . . .

Despite everything, she missed him. She kept telling herself that she ought to be glad he wasn't around, that what she'd heard from his ex was proof she should keep him out of her life. Still . . . his absence left a vacuum that nothing else seemed to fill. Not her work, not the boys, nothing. She longed to see him. She had never been a sports fan and had not taken much interest in golf, even after her short acquaintance with Nick. But now she began to hover near the television set whenever a tournament in which he participated was in progress. And though at first it was just to catch a glimpse of Nick, she soon became caught up in the game, as avid a fan as the boys, holding her breath whenever Nick took a shot, her heart urging him on to victory.

So on the Sunday that Nick McKenzie played in the Western Open at Pebble Beach's prestigious Cypress Point course, Rae was as excited as the boys gathered around the big TV in the family room. By the last round, it was close, with the two top contenders, Nick McKenzie and Doug Powell vying for the championship.

"McKenzie's one down with only three holes to go," the sports announcer informed. "A Powell win if they each par the last three."

"Dad's a shot behind," Kevin said as they watched Powell, a stocky frowning man, approach the tee.

"Don't remind me," Greg moaned. Nick and his opponent tied the next two holes.

That left Nick still one shot behind, Rae thought despondently, and the boys were unnaturally quiet as the announcer made his predictions.

"The eighteenth hole is a par five," he said. "A tough five-hundred-and-sixty-yard dogleg to the left. Looks like a shoo-in for Powell."

Joey jabbed a fist at the commentator. "I don't like him. He's for that other guy."

Rae didn't like him, either.

"A tough one," the announcer repeated grimly.

"Well, like they say, when the going gets tough, the tough get going!" said the other commentator, who had himself been a golf pro. "And McKenzie's tough!"

"He'd better be," responded the network's announcer. "He needs an eagle to win it."

"What's an eagle?" Rae asked. The answer—two under par—depressed her. He was only allowed five strokes to get the ball a long way in one direction and then a long way in another.... It would take more than an eagle, she thought, it would take a miracle.

"Powell's playing it safe," the sports announcer observed as the stocky man took his place on the tee and knocked the ball straight down the fairway. "If he gets a birdie, McKenzie can't win, even with an eagle."

There was a hush on the screen as well as in the living room as Nick came to the tee and measured his stance. How could he look so calm? Rae wondered, watching that half smile, that slow relaxed practice swing. Then a low whistle from the announcer.

"I'll be darned! He's going to cut the corner! Play to win!"

"The only way Nick McKenzie ever plays!" The other commentator was gleeful. "I know. I've played against him."

"What—what does that mean?" Rae asked and Greg hurriedly explained that Nick was going to take a shortcut. Instead of going down the fairway, he planned to knock the ball over "those trees and I don't know what all, plus the distance needed to land on the left fairway for a second shot." An almost impossible task, Greg concluded. "He'll never make it, Mom."

"But it's the only way he can win," Kevin said, his eyes focused anxiously on the screen.

"Yeah." Greg shook his head sadly. "But it'd take superhuman strength to knock it that far."

The whack of the ball could be clearly heard as Nick's swing made contact. The ball sailed up high over the treed rough as if guided by radar, then faded softly to the right.

"A mere hundred yards away." The announcer's voice was filled with awe. "Where does he get that power?"

"He claims he got it hauling hay on his dad's dairy farm," the golf commentator said, grinning.

"He must be a superman," Rae whispered and the boys burst into laughter.

"Yeah! Superman!" Kevin shouted, giving Greg a playful punch. Rae and the boys laughed and applauded, as did the crowd on the screen, rushing forward to watch the second shot. Others hustled to the green area to see the finish.

Rae and the boys gathered closer to the screen for the all-important second shot. Doug Powell hit first, since he was "away," or farthest from the hole.

"A safe, careful three-wood shot, short of the sand trap, sixty yards away from the green," said the broadcaster. "A wedge short-iron shot might mean a birdie."

"Whatever that means," Rae muttered.

"One less than par, Mom," explained Greg. "But for sure he'll make par," he added, and the TV people confirmed it.

Nick selected an eight iron. "Too much club," the commentator cautioned. The ball and a clod of turf left the ground. The sod fell three feet away. The ball sailed high then started its descent and hit the ground with a thud six feet above the hole. A reverse spin began to act, and the ball stopped, "a knee-knocking three feet from the hole," according to the commentator.

"Knee-knocking? Why?" asked Rae.

"Mom, when you're that close you should make it in one stroke. And when you get to thinking about the big bucks hanging on that stroke, your knees begin to knock. Because sometimes you miss," said Greg.

How does he stand it? Rae wondered. *More than my knees would be knocking,* she thought as she watched the other player line up for his birdie putt, roughly six feet away. The camera followed the tap that went straight holeward—then rolled around the back and hung on the lip of the cup. A groan from the crowd, a grimace from Powell.

"No wonder he's grimacing," said the announcer. "If McKenzie makes the knee-knocker, Powell has just dropped eighty thousand dollars, the difference between first and second, and all the perks that follow a win at this prestigious tournament."

And so it was. Nick knocked it in, then threw his ball to the crowd that applauded and yelled its adoration. The camera followed him as he signed his scorecard and continued to the area where the presentation of the trophy and check would take place. There was a short speech by the President of Litcore Corporation, who had sponsored the tournament, and one by the Secretary-General of the PGA.

Rae wasn't listening. How wrong she'd been. This wasn't just a game to be casually enjoyed in the fresh air. Oh, Nick obviously enjoyed playing, but it took skill, planning, risks. Yes, it was a different kind of pressure from what she experienced in her job at the bank, but there was pressure just the same. Again she marveled at Nick's calm.

She watched as Nick graciously accepted his trophy and prize—and was soundly kissed by a stunningly attractive young woman to whom he handed the check! She was so eye-catching that the TV crew asked among themselves for the world to hear, "Who is she?"

The commentator ventured a guess. "A significant other, maybe. Because I do know he's not married."

Rae sat very still, her breathing shallow. She felt devastated—as if something had been snatched from her. The boys disappeared into the kitchen, crowing over the victory. But Rae still stared at the screen, hoping the informational banter would continue after the commercials and the identity of the woman would be disclosed.

Not so. There were only the show's closing credits. Rae felt further let down. She'd been so ecstatic as she witnessed his win. But she'd plummeted to the ground with a thud as she witnessed that kiss and with the world asked, "Who is she?"

ON SUNDAY AFTERNOON a week later, Rae stood at her kitchen sink clearing up the remains of a late lunch. She had just dropped the boys at a nearby movie and the house was quiet except for the rain beating steadily against the kitchen window.

"It's fun to walk in the rain."

She scrubbed vigorously at the sink, trying to shut out the voice that echoed in her mind, the feel of the rain on her face as they splashed through the puddles together. All week long she'd been trying to forget. She had immersed herself in work, determined to shut out all thoughts of Nick.

But she couldn't shut him out. Nor could she banish the image that had for a brief instant flashed on the television screen. The woman, the kiss, the proprietary way in which she took the check. Rae's unaccountable feeling of desolation, of something lost, had persisted despite the anger that began to build. If he had a "significant other," why had he pursued *her?* And why had she responded so avidly?

Being with him was fun, she admitted as she began to pluck dead leaves from the plant on the windowsill. *That* was why. She had loved it. She loved being with him, making him laugh—kissing him. Hot blood rushed to her cheeks and she felt a constriction in her chest as she remembered how he'd looked at her, held her. She had thought their relationship was...well, meaningful.

"My dear, how can you be so naive?" As if in a daze Rae heard the echo of Lady Fraser's cool voice warning her. "Nick avails himself of such opportunities...he turns on the charm."

Rae noticed Rusty settling down at her feet and bent to stroke his soft fur. How could she have thought herself special? Just because he spent a little time with her, flattered and enticed her.... Oh, she was a fool! Thank God she hadn't stayed in Monterey.

"His women" Jan had said. Of course. Nick was a handsome, virile, famous man. Of course he would attract women, beautiful, seductive, sexy women.

Rae stood quite still, her fingers tightly gripping the edge of the sink. The picture was still clear in her mind. The stunning blonde tossing back her hair, lifting in-

viting lips and flinging her arms around Nick. She was
no groupie and he wasn't beating her off with his club,
either. He had slipped his arm around her and—

No, she would not think of Nick McKenzie. He
was a deceitful— The ringing doorbell cut into her
thoughts.

She opened the door and he stood there, that lopsided all's-right-with-the-world smile on his lips.
"Hello, Rae."

"Hi."

"Good boy, Rusty," he said absently as he wiped his
feet on the doormat and shook the raindrops from his
hair. "What's going on?" he asked, hanging his jacket
in the closet just as if he hadn't been away, as if he
hadn't been so publicly kissed.

"Same old thing," she answered, pleased at how
nonchalant she sounded. "We've just been marking
time while you were out winning money and laurels."
And no telling what else.

"Had a little bit of luck!" he sang, giving a good
imitation of Mr. Doolittle in *My Fair Lady*. "Where are
the boys?"

"At the movies. And it wasn't all luck at Pebble
Beach." She had to give him that. "I saw you knock
that ball over the trees."

His eyes lighted with pleasure. "You watched?"

She nodded. "And the words I heard were skill and
power, for which I shall reward you with a cup of coffee." *Not a kiss,* she thought with bitter irony.

"Luck," he insisted. "I could have landed in the
bunker. But I'll take the coffee," he added, then followed her to the kitchen.

"How about lunch?" she asked, determined to be hospitable, but cool and detached. "There's potato salad and some ham."

"Sounds great, which the airline's food was not," he said, sliding into the booth at the breakfast table.

They seemed to have run out of words. She was uncomfortably aware of his eyes. They seemed to question her as she moved about, placing croissants in the oven and taking out the salad she had just put away. She had to say something.

"Maybe you'd better slice this," she said, unwrapping the ham.

Still silent, he got up and did so.

She filled his plate, took the croissants from the oven, poured coffee for both of them.

"Your...er...Lady Fraser paid us a visit," she said as she sat and sipped her coffee.

"So I heard."

"Kevin?"

"He caught me in Miami. Terribly upset because she wants him to quit his job. Ridiculous. I told him to keep it if he wants to. Great salad," he said over a hefty forkful.

"Thank you." Rae was still thinking of Lady Fraser. "She seemed so...so determined."

Nick shrugged. "He's keeping up his grades, he loves the job, and he's old enough to make his own decisions. And I don't want to talk about that," he declared suddenly, putting down his napkin. "Miscalculation all cleared up?"

"Miscalculation?"

"The one that required your presence at the bank. Surely you haven't forgotten so soon."

"Oh, no. I mean, yes," she replied in utter confusion, angry that he'd sprung it on her like this. She had hoped he wouldn't bring it up.

"Or perhaps there's some other, as-yet-undisclosed reason you deserted me?"

She almost choked on her coffee. It would be so embarrassing if he ever guessed— "What..what do you mean?"

"I mean the eminent Mr. Bowers must appreciate your diligence."

"Bowers?" What did he have to do with anything?

"He's your boss or romantic interest or both, isn't he? He certainly seems to require an exorbitant amount of your time." His coolly disapproving voice was edged with anger and she stared at him in amazement. "Oh, hell, I didn't intend to attack you like this," he said roughly. "But when you left me without a word of explanation, I was so..." He swallowed. "Well, it upset me. And confused me. Don't you think it's time you were honest with me, Rae?"

His tone sparked her anger. "Honest with you?"

"Yes. I never thought of you as a tease. And I don't appreciate your leading me on."

Leading *him* on! How dare he! The image that had haunted her all week flashed before her like a bolt of lightning and she retorted vehemently, "Well, I don't appreciate your not being honest with me!"

"Just what do you mean by that?"

"I mean you came on with all that talk about wanting to be part of my life so you could be near Kevin."

"Yes. That was true," he said and his innocent puzzled look really made her irate.

"But you also had something else in mind. You wanted to go to bed—" She broke off, appalled at herself. "Oh, you know what you had in mind!"

He gave her a level stare. "Yes. And it wasn't all in *my* mind, either."

"Well, you can just forget it, Nick McKenzie! I don't intend to join the flock of...of one-night wonders you deserted your wife for!"

"Oho! So my manipulative ex had a chat with you as well as Kevin!"

"We...we had lunch and a most informative talk."

"Informative? You mean you swallowed all her lies and innuendos?"

"Are you denying that you deserted her?"

"Hell, yes! I did not desert her or my marriage. I quit, fair and square. I ran as one would from a rattlesnake." They faced each other across the table like two combatants, and his voice rose. "Nor did I desert my son. I—no, we—dissolved that farce of a marriage. It has nothing to do with Kevin."

"Are you denying the one-nighters?"

"Yes. And I resent the implication." His expression was so stormy that for a moment she was frightened. He pushed his plate back and seemed to be trying to get control of himself. "All right. I'm no celibate. I enjoy the companionship of women, and there have been a few. But I'll tell you one thing—it's *always* been by mutual consent. It was always understood that either party could walk away at any time." He stood up and looked down at her, adding with emphasis, "No one has to *run*."

Nick put his cup down. He strode to the front door and out of it without another word.

CHAPTER TWELVE

NICK CALMED DOWN as he drove home. Rae had been bombarded with a pack of Jan's lies. Jan was a vindictive witch! Would he never be rid of her vicious meddling?

As for Rae . . . she was an enigma, and he had to admit he was attracted. She was witty, delightful company, intelligent, and damn good-looking. And a good mother through and through. The environment of her home was so right for his son.

And now here was Jan sticking her nose in! Demanding that Kevin give up a job he loved because she considered it beneath him. Oh yes, he knew that lady. She had never wanted him to reveal that his folks were common farmers. He laughed out loud as he remembered how she had begged him to dig up that title that had been buried for years. Seemed to think he could dust it off and wear it like a halo that would admit them into what she considered "the right circles." He'd gone through a bit of hell over that stupid idea. Jan would go to any lengths to get her own way.

He frowned. She would go to any lengths, even hauling Kevin back to England, to get her own way. Maybe Kevin *should* quit that job. After all, it was only a few hours a week.

No! It was the principle of the thing. Kevin had to learn to deal with her, learn to make his own decisions. He, Nick McKenzie, would see that his son was free to do so! Nobody was going to pressure the boy against his own healthy, decent inclinations.

He'd definitely keep in close touch, though he was going to be on tour for the next few weeks. He had been invited to play Spy Glass in California, The Dunes in Nevada, and Dorel in Florida. But he'd have some time off before the Masters in Augusta, and he'd try to schedule something for Kevin and himself, and the Pascal boys if their mother would let them. Of course she would! He'd have Elaine set it up.

As for Rae... She shouldn't be pressured against her inclinations either, he thought as he pulled into his carport and shut off the engine. He sat for a full minute, staring into space, feeling as bereft as he had that day in Monterey when he returned to the hotel and found her gone.

SHE WANTED TO RUN after him and call him back. She hadn't meant the ugly words she had said. At least not all of them. She knew he hadn't moved here because of her. It was because of Kevin. He really cared about Kevin. The time he devoted to him—yes, and to her boys—proved that.

And suppose he was...well, attracted to her. She was attracted to him, wasn't she? He hadn't been pushy, had always acceded to her wishes. It wasn't his fault that she wasn't...couldn't...was such a dud.

She looked at his half-finished lunch and admitted that the words she'd uttered had been in self-defense. She hadn't wanted her own inadequacies exposed and had tried to shift the blame onto him.

Not that he was entirely blameless, though. Jan had said— No, she had only half believed the things Lady

Fraser had said. Even though, as she'd listened, she had heard her own experiences with Tom played all over again. Dear Lord, Tom had been dead for nine years and she had to stop letting him influence her life! In her heart she knew that Nick wasn't like Tom. He was open and honest.

But she hadn't been honest with him. She had lied about why she'd left Monterey. And today... hiding behind that lie, she had sat there parroting Lady Fraser's insinuations, skirting the question she had harbored all week. Who was that woman who'd kissed him? What was she to him?

He would probably have told her.

She hadn't asked. Because she was afraid of the answer.

Still, she was sorry she'd spoken to him as she had. She would apologize if she got the chance.

The chance never came during the days that followed. They weren't on the same friendly footing, and there never seemed to be an opportunity. He was away most of the time and when he wasn't... well, somehow he managed to avoid her.

He kept in touch with the boys, though, especially Kevin. Kevin was going through a bad time. His mother had called three times and was indignant that he hadn't quit his job. The third call had been to Rae.

"My dear, for some reason Kevin has not yet discontinued his association with that veterinary facility. I wish you'd see to it immediately."

"Lady Fraser, it's only a few hours a week," So much ado about such a small thing. No, not small to Kevin. "He really enjoys it, and in fact, he's focused on—"

"On not following my instructions," Lady Fraser had snapped.

"No, on a career as a veterinarian. And they've taken quite an interest in Kevin at the college, letting him observe operations and so on. His father thinks—"

"His father has nothing to do with it! I expect you to see that Kevin follows my wishes."

Her wishes. Not his own. "Lady Fraser, it's hardly my place—"

"It certainly is your place, and I am depending on you, my dear. Surely as a mother you understand how I feel. I must ring off now, but you may call me when you've taken care of it. I do so appreciate your help, my dear." She'd hung up before Rae could voice further protests.

Rae's lips tightened as she recalled the conversation. She didn't like being given an ultimatum. And it certainly was *not* her place to make a happy boy unhappy. Maybe she should discuss it with Nick—if he ever spoke to her again. But it was Kevin who approached her with the problem.

"Mother's insisting I give up my job," he told her. "I don't want to. I like it and—" he hesitated "—I think they like me. And since I'll be applying for college here—"

"Oh, Kevin, I'm glad." She hadn't known that he intended to apply. "We love having you with us. And I agree with you. I mean... Oh, I don't think the job is interfering with your studies. Perhaps you should talk the matter over with your father." *Unlike your mother, he seems to have your interests at heart.*

Meanwhile, Leon Waters had scheduled a meeting in L.A., specifically requesting that she attend with Harrison Bowers. Something was about to break and she felt edgy. She didn't know why. Usually she felt calm and secure about whatever happened at work.

"Mom," Joey said, appearing at her elbow. "Todd says they've got skateboards on sale at—"

"I don't care where they're on sale," she snapped irritably. "I told you I'm not buying you a skateboard at this time." He was still loaded with things he'd received for Christmas.

"You bought Greg new basketball shoes."

"I did not. He bought them himself with money he earned."

"But nobody's going to give me a job. I'm just a ten-year-old kid."

"Yeah, well, that's tough," she said, almost laughing. Then she rumpled his hair and crooned, "Rest your little head upon my shoulder, wait till you get a little bit older!" He jerked away and ran to his room, and immediately she regretted her behavior. She shouldn't tease him. Maybe she ought to buy him the skateboard. No, she had to be firm about not spoiling him and if he couldn't take a little teasing . . . Oh, for heaven's sake, what was the matter with her? Anxious about every little thing. The meeting in L.A., Kevin, Joey . . .

She knew. Underlying everything was the agony of missing Nick. Maybe if she heard him whistling or saw his relaxed, confident smile, things wouldn't get so . . . so out of proportion. Everything would be lighthearted and fun again. She wished she hadn't alienated him. But would that have made any difference? He'd still be on tour. She couldn't help wondering if that woman was with him again. Rae hadn't watched the Spy Glass tournament. The boys said he came in second, but she hadn't wanted to see and hadn't asked if he'd been kissed.

She took a deep breath and shrugged. Fun or not, life went on and she'd better start packing. They'd probably have to stay overnight in L.A.

HE WAITED UNTIL after eight to phone because he knew Rae would be home by then. Elaine had suggested he invite the boys for the Masters tournament, instead of the weekend before. They'd be out of school for Easter break then. He had purposefully avoided all contact with Rae and meant to continue doing so. All he wanted now was to get her permission and to coordinate schedules. So why did he feel as nervous as a kid about to ask for his first date? As the phone began to ring his heart pounded crazily and he couldn't believe how eager he was just to hear her voice.

"Hello." Joey. He felt let down.

"Hi, Joey. What's going on?"

"Nothing. Are you home, Nick? Coming over?"

"No. I'm in Reno. I wanted to ask—"

"Aw, I thought you were back. We saw you Sunday. We wanted you to win. Greg said if the other guy had missed that putt—"

"Yes, that was too bad. Listen, Joey, where's your...everybody?"

"Greg and Kevin went to a band concert at their school and Ms. Steele's in the bath. She told me to answer the phone."

"Ms. Steele?"

"Yeah, she's staying with us on account of Mom's not here. Mr. Bowers picked her up early this morning and she's in L.A. Nick! What's that? What's that noise, Nick?"

"Nothing, Joey. Just...er...dropped my drink. Clumsy of me." Bowers. L.A. Well, hell! If she was going to keep up these overnighters she ought to be better prepared. Get a regular housekeeper instead of scraping up some friend or other. Damn messy way of doing things. Not that he gave a damn *how* many nights she was away—or with whom!

"Nick, are you still there?"

"Yes, Joey. Yes. Look. Good to talk with you. I'll be in touch, okay?" He hung up the phone. Hell, he didn't need to talk to Rae. He'd have Elaine call and arrange the whole thing.

RAE COULD FEEL Harrison Bowers watching her as the flight attendant ushered them to their spacious seats in first class, stored their jackets and asked if they'd like drinks while the other passengers were boarding. Both declined and when the attendant left them, Harrison said what had evidently been on his mind all afternoon.

"You don't look like someone who's just received the prize offer of the year."

"I know." Rae sighed, remembering Waters's shocked expression when she'd told them she'd have to think about it. Now she looked at Bowers. "I know refusing an offer like this is simply not done, but Harrison, I don't want a figurehead V.P. spot at Corporate."

"V.P. for foreign loans and investments is hardly a figurehead position."

"I know."

"And think of the perks. You'd be making a world-wide tour with the Chairman of the Board at least once a year, not to mention the usual dinners, the travel, the contacts. Incredible exposure for anyone who wants to get ahead."

"Agreed. Figurehead was wrong. But travel isn't what I want. And I don't want to be in L.A. I want to be where I am." She thought of Greg in his junior year, at last buckling down to his studies, happy with his teammates. Joey, happy with his friends. It was the wrong time to uproot them. "Don't you see? I have two boys to raise."

"I know. But, Rae, in our business, you either lead, follow or get out of the way. You've always done, and you continue to do, a good job for Coastal. That offer proves tokenism is not their game. And, as your immediate supervisor, I would advise you to think very carefully about an outright refusal. Okay?"

At that point the preliminaries of preflight were finished and the whine of the jet engines at full thrust put a temporary stop to further conversation.

As the airplane climbed and finally leveled off, Rae thought about what Bowers had said and decided he was right on every point. She was about to say so when he spoke again.

"Maybe," he said softly, "you're more a mother than a banker. And what you really need is a husband, not a promotion." That had an amorous sound and she was about to retort when he placed a finger over her mouth. "That wasn't a pitch. We know where I fit in your life. What I said was simply a sincere observation from a guy who thinks you're terrific. But, Rae, you can't have your cake and eat it, too."

The seldom-speechless Rae Pascal was now just that. She squirmed in her seat, sighed and finally murmured, "You're right, Harrison, but up to now I could handle my career and my children. And, honestly, I think I could still do it if I'm allowed to remain in Dansby."

Harrison nodded and shrugged his shoulders, then turned toward the window, adjusting his pillow to nap. "The catch is *if you're allowed.*"

Rae sat for a moment blinking back tears. It had been a long time since she'd cried. But now...well, darn it, if she wanted to cry, why not? She unbuckled her seat belt, went into the rest room and bolted the door. Sitting there, she let the tears flow unchecked. She felt very foolish. She didn't even know why she was crying. It was just that suddenly things seemed so unsettled. Undecided. She enjoyed her work at the bank and had always been pleased when she was upgraded. But now... Bowers was right. After you reached a certain level nothing was static. You went up, over, or out—at the bank's convenience, not yours. And what about the boys? Was she being too protective? This was a mobile society and her sons had to learn to adjust.

Or was it herself she was protecting? Clinging to the home where she'd spent a happy childhood. And where, during the past four months, she had come close to a greater happiness....

That was it. That was why she was crying. Because she couldn't bear to face what she had lost. And she didn't know whether she'd lost him because of her own failings or because a beautiful blond woman had the right to fling her arms around him and—

Rae sat up, dried her tears. Any exuberant bystander could have rushed up and kissed him. It didn't have to be...

He had handed her his check.

Now Rae felt like laughing. Idiot that she was, she'd hardly thought about the check. That was more important than the kiss. The woman had to be close to him. Pretty darn close to have charge of his winnings!

Rae was shocked by the rage that gripped her. She wasn't sure whether it was at Nick or herself. Stupid of her to sit here bawling over a man who was that close to someone else!

The anger helped. She was once again the self-possessed, self-sufficient Rae Pascal. She had her career and her boys. Nothing else mattered. She would take her time, think things over, make the right decision.

She fixed her makeup and returned to seat 3B.

When she reached home, all three boys crowded around her, beside themselves with excitement, all talking at once.

"Wait. One at a time, please," she begged.

"Dad called," said Kevin. "He wants me, Greg and Joey—if you'll let them—to join him in Augusta for the Masters tournament."

She was besieged by a chorus of "it's all right with you, isn't it?" and "we can go, can't we?" Greg pointed out that it would be during Easter break so they wouldn't miss school. She soon got it all sorted out and of course gave her consent. Amid the yells of exultation Kevin managed to convey that a Ms. Cummings would call her about the arrangements.

A few days later she did receive a call from Ms. Cummings, a pleasant-sounding woman whom Rae assumed to be a travel agent. It was five weeks before the tournament, but Ms. Cummings had already arranged flight schedules and hotel accommodations, and Mr. McKenzie had asked her to check with Mrs. Pascal to see if these were satisfactory. Rae said they were and thanked her.

That was thoughtful of Nick. It was always difficult to plan for the time during vacation and holidays when she was at work and the boys were out of school. And this, she told herself, was a special treat for them. To be there, on the scene at a Masters Tournament! They would love it.

There was no reason she should have been included in the invitation. No reason, either, for the depression that plagued her. She worked harder than ever at the office, continually weighing the pros and cons of a move to the Corporate office. But she couldn't seem to shake a strange feeling of sadness and longing.

The mood seemed to lift whenever Nick was in town. Hope? Anticipation? That was foolish, for she only caught brief glimpses of him when he came for the boys; he never lingered at the house. She knew it was his busiest season and he was usually in Dansby for only one or two days between tournaments. Yet he never failed to call the boys from wherever he happened to be.

"Dad told me just to concentrate on what I want and go after it," reported Kevin who still received demanding phone calls from his mother every week or two. "He says if you decide what you want and work hard enough at it, you'll succeed."

Does that apply to relationships, too? Rae wondered. If she worked at regaining her relationship with Nick... But how could she do that if she never saw him?

"Nick said you were right, Mom." Joey told her one day with a sheepish look. "He said you can't expect people to give you everything you want. You have to work for it. And I'm gonna earn money and get my own skateboard."

"Oh, yeah?" Greg chuckled derisively. "Somebody offer you a job?"

"Nope. I'm in business for myself," Joey said proudly. "See? I already got five dollars." To their astonishment he displayed the money and revealed he had earned it by wading in the knee-high water hazard to recover golf balls, which he had then sold to golfers at the club. "Nick okayed it with Mr. Johnson, the manager, Mom. And Mr. Johnson says I can come anytime, even if Nick's not there. Can you take me on Saturday, Mom? 'Cause Nick's leaving tomorrow night and he won't be back for a real long time."

Rae nodded, smiling. She looked at her baby who was "going into business" and no longer sulking about what she wouldn't give him. *Nick.* It was his doing. And she was grateful.

She suddenly had an overwhelming desire to tell him so. Right now. Joey's words—"he won't be back for a real long time"—echoed in her ears.

Did she feel more than gratitude? Was this an attempt to regain their old relationship? Perhaps. At least friendship, if nothing else, and she did want to thank him as well as erase the ugly words she'd said.

"I'm taking off a little early today," she told Cora as she gathered up her things. She had no idea when Nick was scheduled to leave. Joey said tonight, but maybe if she hurried . . .

NICK OPENED HIS DOOR and was surprised to see his accountant and close friend, Elaine Cummings, standing on his doorstep, suitcase and briefcase beside her.

"I tried to get hold of you to let you know I was coming, but you don't stay in one place long enough."

She tossed back her blond hair and grinned at him. "Well, aren't you going to let me in? After I came all the way from Miami?"

"Oh, sure. Come on in," he said as he picked up the suitcase. "I just made coffee. But what's a good-lookin' gal like you doin' all alone in this here neck of the woods?" he asked in an exaggerated cowboy drawl.

"Chasing *you* down."

"Well, here I am." He did a little soft-shoe routine that made her laugh. "Now, what's going on?" he asked, in a more serious tone. Despite her beauty, Elaine was all business. And there must be some serious concern, for she didn't relish surprise visits any more than he did.

"Preferred stockholders' meeting in San Francisco. I just got a forty-eight hour notice. Where's that coffee?"

"Coming up. Follow me."

She followed him into the kitchen, carrying the briefcase. "Remember the ball team and sports complex you authorized me to invest in?"

"The Monarchs. I thought they were going well."

"They are. But an unfriendly takeover is in the wind and all principal shareholders are required for a briefing in Sacramento tomorrow. So you and I have to talk."

"By all means. Let's talk and decide. I'll have to sign proxy papers because, as you know, I'm due at Dorel tomorrow."

"Yes, I do. That's why I rushed." She took the mug of coffee he offered, sat at the table and opened her briefcase. "I didn't even make a hotel reservation. Better call now."

"Stay here. Four bedrooms. Take your choice."

"Thanks. That'll be convenient. Four bedrooms, huh? Much larger than your place in Florida. Lots of room for just you—and your son, I presume?" She lifted one eyebrow significantly.

"Stop presuming. Kevin and the Pascal boys like to bring their friends over."

"I see. It's been good for you, having him this year, hasn't it? Well, let's get cracking." She took papers from her case. They discussed options and alternatives, then reached a decision. The proxy papers were signed. After that, he briefed her on the surrounding area, finished his packing, left his keys for her to use the car and took a cab to the airport.

RAE FELT NERVOUS as she turned into the club grounds. It was almost five and he might be gone. But when she pulled up in front of his house she saw his car. He was there.

Now she was even more nervous.

She rang the bell.

No answer.

She rang again.

Elaine, who had just entered the shower stall, heard the bell and thought, "Oh, Nick forgot something. And I've got his keys." She grabbed a towel, wrapped it around herself and shouted, "I'm coming, Nick."

Had she gone to the wrong place? Rae checked the number.

No. Right number. All of a sudden, she wanted to run.

But by then it was too late. The latch was disengaged and the door opened wide. The two women stared at each other, speechless.

They spoke together. One said, "Oh, I thought you were Nick."

And the other, "Oh, I was looking for Mr. Mc—"

Then they started again, Elaine first. "Oh, please come in. As you can see, I was in the shower. You must be Rae Pascal."

Rae managed a drunken entry and a feeble "Yes."

Elaine moved toward the bathroom and said over her shoulder, "You must have passed Nick. He's only been gone five or ten minutes. I'll be right out. I'm Elaine Cummings, by the way. I talked with you on the phone and, in fact, I was planning to visit you during my stay. Excuse me while I get dressed."

Rae was grateful for the delay. Time to pull herself together. The mystery woman was no longer a mystery. She was here, alive and well. Blond and beautiful. *Younger than me,* Rae thought.

She felt an overwhelming sense of shock and devastation.

From all appearances, this woman was a permanent party. No stranger. No one-nighter.

In a sudden frenzy of helpless fury, Rae wondered if this Elaine had always been in the picture. She thought again about her sophomoric retreat from that cosy inn in Monterey. Now she told herself her action had been prophetic and wise.

Elaine entered, brushing her hair, explaining her hectic trip from Florida. What a relief that she'd caught Nick just in time. And how fortunate that Rae had dropped in.

"I wanted to assure you that you don't need to be concerned about your sons at the Masters. I'll be there and I plan to keep my eye on them as well as on Kevin."

"Thank you. I appreciate that," Rae said, not betraying by the blink of an eye that knowing this stunning woman would "be there" was like a knife in her heart.

"I'm glad to do it. The airline tickets have already been ordered and I'll see that you get them a week in advance. Oh, dear, I'm not being very hospitable. Would you like a cup of coffee? Or a drink?"

"No. No thank you. No time. Another pressing engagement," Rae lied and hastily made ready to leave.

"I'm sorry you missed Nick," said the remarkably beautiful woman. "Would you like me to give him a message? I'll be talking to him tomorrow night."

"No, thank you. It was just... nothing important. No need to bother him." *And no need to mention that I came by.* But she couldn't tell Elaine that, no matter how much she wanted to, Rae thought as she made a polite, if rather hurried, departure.

Driving home, Rae was annoyed with herself. That should teach her to go running after Nick!

She hadn't dared to ask him, but today she'd come face-to-face with his mystery woman. Elaine Cummings was obviously, as the commentator had said, a significant other. *Very* significant!

CHAPTER THIRTEEN

THE NEXT DAY Bowers was still urging her to take the job at Corporate. "You can't vacillate on a thing like this, Rae. There's a long list of eager applicants. You know that."

She did know it, but she still had two weeks to decide and she needed to think long and hard. "I'm considering it," she told him.

"Consider it well," he said. "I told you you can't have your cake and eat it, too. If you turn this down, you might be blackballed from any further advancement."

She knew that, and the job tempted her. The raise in pay was certainly an inducement with Greg only two years away from college. But the constant travel would require her to get a live-in housekeeper to stay with the boys. Could she find a really reliable person? And living in Los Angeles—such a *huge* city with all the attendant vices and problems. She liked the atmosphere of the relatively quiet little college town of Dansby.

So she continued to vacillate.

As for Nick McKenzie, she had resolved not to think about him. It was a hard resolution to keep; starting Thursday, the first day of the Heritage Tournament, he had been featured on every television sports program. Greg and Kevin had tuned in to each one and, much against her will, Rae found she couldn't stay away from the set. It was now Sunday afternoon, and today's broadcast featured the final round. Nick and Ron Davis, one of the three remaining competitors, were tied at twelve under par. Rae, like the two boys, was glued to the set as the game progressed and the tie held.

"One thing about Nick McKenzie," the announcer said, "no matter how badly or how well things are going, he never loses his cool."

Rae marveled that this was true. Watching that loose graceful stride to the tee, his relaxed stance, the gentle yet confident smile, she felt her heart warm to him. He had an easy way of handling things, a light touch—disciplining or playing with the boys, fixing a leak or repairing a broken lawn chair. Saving her dinner party. Competing in a major golf tournament on worldwide television. Yes, that was Nick.

When she'd called at his home and come face-to-face with Elaine Cummings, Rae had been embarrassed and angry. The anger had disappeared, leaving in its place what felt like a gaping hole, painful to the touch. And so she'd shied away from any thought of Nick.

Now, as she watched him on TV, the thoughts flooded her mind and she recalled every incident in their short relationship. This was a man who, from the moment they'd met, had been like a father to her boys. Who had awakened in her wonderful exhilarating emotions that had been buried for years. The gaping hole filled and overflowed with love. Pure, unequivocal, unselfish love. She wanted this man to be happy, even if it was with another woman. She sat watching every hole of the tournament, excited and tense, praying for him to win.

He didn't. At hole seventeen, a par five dogleg left, with a water hazard, Nick opted to chance the water, hoping to make the green on two. Kevin and Greg groaned and Rae winced as Nick's ball rolled into the trap. But, Rae mused, Nick never lost his cool. His interview with the sportscaster was jovial and upbeat, and his second-place share of the winnings amounted to eighty-five thousand dollars.

"Not bad," Greg said with a grin, "for three days' work at something you really enjoy."

That statement sent Rae's mind reeling. "Something you really enjoy." Loans and investments was the area of her work that intrigued her and, according to Waters, the area in which she had gained a special expertise. The position of Vice President, Foreign Loans and Investments, would be an exciting challenge, one she'd enjoy.

But she enjoyed her boys, too, enjoyed watching their progress and their play. She wanted to be with them during their growing years. Maybe Harrison was right. She was more a mother than a banker.

Anyway, she still had a week to decide.

Monday afternoon, Nick returned to Dansby. He called Kevin and suggested a late dinner; he also invited Greg to join them.

"Okay, Mom?" Greg asked.

"Sure." She wanted him to be with Nick as often as he could in the little time that was left. Kevin would be leaving in June and so, she imagined, would Nick.

She was sorry the boys were downstairs, ready and waiting, when Nick came to pick them up. She had hoped for a minute alone with him. She wanted to say some of the things she had intended to say the day she'd gone to his place and he was gone. She also wanted to commiserate with him over his loss in South Carolina.

But the boys were there and they crowded around him, both talking at once. Nick's greeting to her was so cold and formal that she was devastated, and whatever she might have said stuck in her throat.

However, just as they were about to depart, she did manage a word of condolence about his loss. "That was a heartbreaker. You were so close."

Her words were met with a cavalier shrug. "Not to worry. You win, and then when you least expect it, you lose. I lost in South Carolina, won in Florida, and," he said, looking directly at her, "lost a hard one in Monterey." His words hung in the air as he went out.

She stared at the closed door, hearing Kevin's "When did you lose in Monterey, Dad?"

She didn't know how Nick answered him but she knew he hadn't been referring to golf. And the way he'd looked at her... Regret? Hurt?

Oh, good heavens. There she went again. Trying to make something significant out of a few words, a look. If he wanted to repair the relationship, he would have asked *her* to dinner, not the boys. Her sigh was one of resignation. Any idea she'd had about his interest in her had been fully dismissed during this past month.

She'd have to be on her guard not to make a fool of herself when he was here to see the boys, she thought as she glanced at her watch. Time to pick up Joey from Cub Scouts.

When she returned a half hour later, the phone was ringing. She caught it on the fourth ring, almost tripping over Rusty in her dash to the kitchen.

"I was about to hang up," said Jan Fraser. Rae answered that she'd just come in and Jan said she was glad she hadn't missed her. "I don't want to spring any surprises on you. I rang to tell you I've arranged for

Kevin to return home. He has reservations on Intercontinental. The flight leaves on Friday at—"

"Friday? But surely you can't mean that! School isn't over until June."

"I am aware of that, but this quarter is almost over. I'm sure his credits can be transferred and he can continue his schooling here."

"I don't understand," Rae said. What did the woman mean—"not springing any surprises"? "This is so sudden. Is there some emergency?"

"No emergency. I am sorry, Mrs. Pascal, but since you have allowed Kevin to utterly disregard my wishes, I think it best to remove him from your charge."

Damn the woman! Was this really about Kevin's job or was she just determined to get her own way? "But Lady Fraser, I told you it wasn't my place to make that kind of decision. It's between Kevin and his..." She checked herself. Any mention of Nick always set her off.

"Perhaps you're right, my dear. I realize you're in an awkward position. And I hope you will not regard my action as pique at you. You have been most gracious. Kevin tells me he has so much enjoyed his stay." Lady Fraser seemed to regret her initial sharpness and now rattled off a string of polite nothings.

Rae wasn't listening. She was trying to think of something that would dissuade this spiteful woman from snatching Kevin away. "I do wish you would reconsider. He only has a few more weeks and my boys will be so disappointed to see him leave now. They've made plans for the Easter break in April—"

"I am aware of that!" The brittle tone was back. "And to tell you the truth, Mrs. Pascal, I am not pleased. I have never permitted Kevin to attend such

functions. The crowd, the atmosphere, is not condu-
cive to... to his betterment.''

So that was it! Not the crowds, nor the atmosphere.
Not even the job. It was his father. For some reason of
her own, this vicious woman wanted Kevin to be estranged from Nick. No wonder those two had been like
strangers to each other. Jan's doing. And if she had her
way, she would force them apart again.

That would be a shame, especially now that they'd
become so close.

"Do you really think this is a wise move?'' she
countered, struggling to sound reasonable and composed. "To be chosen as a foreign exchange student is
a privilege and an honor, an impressive item on future
applications or résumés. I'd hate to see Kevin's record
spoiled. There's sure to be some question about an
abrupt departure in the middle of the year.''

"My dear, you should not make the mistake of un-
derestimating our status. There will never be any
question about the qualifications of *my* son, the son of
Lord and Lady Fraser.'' Her pompous tone, as well as
the sheer audacity of the statement, made Rae's skin
crawl with indignation. "My decision is irrevocable. I
have notified the coordinator of foreign exchange stu-
dents in your area and he will be in touch with you.
This is simply a courtesy call to give you prior notice.
I must ring off now. Thank you again for your kind-
ness and cooperation.'' Without another word Lady
Fraser broke the connection.

Shocked, Rae glanced down at the phone, still tightly
clutched in her hand. She slammed it down in a burst
of the fury she was unable to vent on Lady Fraser. She
now had a clear picture of the woman's shrewishness,

her senseless bias, and she understood why Nick had walked away.

But Kevin couldn't walk away. He was still subject to her vicious whims. For some reason, she was self-ishly determined to undermine Nick's relationship with his son.

Rae's breath came short as rage and resolution knotted inside her. *A father has rights, too, whether you know it or not, Lady Fraser. And I will do everything in my power to keep those two together!*

But what *could* she do, other than to warn Nick as soon as he returned?

Later, as soon as she heard the boys bounding in the door, she rushed to catch him, only to find he'd dropped them off and driven away. Just as well, she thought. Kevin shouldn't be privy to their conversation.

She waited a reasonable time, then called his home. No answer.

She waited anxiously. It was important that she reach him immediately; there were only a few days left to halt Kevin's departure. She called again. Still no answer. It was late, very late. A sharp streak of jealousy shot through her. Had he gone to join Elaine Cummings—or perhaps another woman with whom he was spending the night? After all, what did Rae know about his involvements? The jealousy made her feel physically ill and kept her awake most of the night. But it didn't dim her resolution. Her own hurt faded beside her concern for Nick and Kevin.

When she called again early the next morning and still received no answer, she casually questioned the boys. Had Nick left for another tournament?

No, they told her, he'd decided to skip the next PGA event to rest and train for the Hawaiian Open.

At her office she repeatedly tried to reach him but with no success. He must be on the golf course—or so she hoped. Finally at ten o'clock she left a message on his answering machine, requesting that he call her regarding important news from Jan.

A half hour later, Cora buzzed her. "A Ms. Cummings on the line, Rae."

So that *was* where he'd gone. And he must have checked his messages. "Let me talk to her," she said, stifling the resentment.

"Hello, Mrs. Pascal. This is Elaine Cummings. I'm sorry to bother you at work, but I needed to check with you about—oh, hold on, would you please?" Rae heard a muffled "All right, darling," and then—a kiss? Finally a "Yes, I'll be here" before Elaine's clear voice came back over the wire. "Sorry about the interruption. Listen, there's been a change in the flight schedule. The boys will be leaving a day earlier and I wanted to check with you before—"

"Oh, yes, fine. But wait, I need to talk to you about something else. Or rather I need to talk with Nick, if you don't mind." They had not received her message. But at least she'd got hold of him, Rae thought, as she waited for Elaine to put him on.

"Has something come up? Excuse me again, please," This time the aside was "Right there on the bureau, dear." Then she was back. "Husbands! He's always losing his keys." Husbands? Nick? Rae's confused mind raced with hurt and disappointment, but she tried again.

"Ms. Cummings, will you please tell Nick that I have to talk to him. Immediately."

"Yes, of course. But you'll probably see him before I do." Elaine Cummings sounded puzzled. "If not, I'll be in touch and I'll give him the message. Let's see, he's probably on a plane now, but he should be back in Dansby sometime this afternoon. Can I help in any way? You sound upset. I do hope you're not thinking of canceling the boys' trip."

"No. I don't want to cancel. But..." Rae's voice faded as she tried to pull her thoughts together. Nick was on a plane. Some other man was Elaine's husband. But why had she been in Nick's shower, in his bathrobe? Rae felt weak and shaken. "Lady Fraser called me last night and I've been trying to reach him. I left a message and when you called I thought perhaps he was with you."

"No. He left for Reno last night. One of his favorite caddies was involved in an automobile accident and Nick went to see him. It turned out to be not as serious as reported and he's on his way back. You say Jan called? Is there trouble again?"

Again? Rae wondered how much Elaine knew of Nick's affairs. "She... well, she's made arrangements for Kevin to return to England on Friday."

"Friday? This week? She probably heard Kevin was going with Nick to the Masters."

"I think that was it," said Rae. So Elaine did know.

"Ms. Pascal, you may not be aware of it, but the McKenzies' divorce was anything but friendly. As his accountant and financial advisor, I know how much Nick has paid, ostensibly for his son's support and education. And I rather suspect that Jan does whatever she can to subvert the relationship between Nick and Kevin."

In one fell swoop, Rae was elated, thankful and encouraged. If Elaine Cummings had been there in person, she would have hugged her. She wasn't Nick's lover! She was a happily married woman, a good friend, and she looked after his money. What was more, she was fully aware that Lady Fraser was a vindictive witch, although she voiced it in more polite terms.

"You must tell him about Jan's threats as soon as he returns," said Elaine.

"Oh, I will. I will. And thank you." *Thank you for not being part of Nick's life. At least not the part I thought you were. The part I want to be.*

These same thoughts were a repetitious jumble in her mind and she kept remembering Nick's prophetic words that night in the parking lot—"I want to become part of your life." Was there a chance? Did he still care? That look in his eyes when he said "I lost a hard one in Monterey." Maybe, maybe... Her whole body vibrated in an ecstasy of longing and hope that almost diminished her anxiety about Kevin.

By the time Nick's call came, she was so keyed up she could hardly speak. "Oh, Nick," she sputtered, "I've been trying to reach you. I tried to stop you when you came back from dinner and then when I called you—"

"Sorry. I left as soon as I got home. A message about Ted, a caddy. But, you said Jan called?" he asked and she heard the unmistakable apprehension. "What's up?"

She told him.

"Damn it! Well, this time she has bloody well gone too far!" There was a pause and when he spoke again, it was with cool resolve. "Not to worry. I'll take care of this. Kevin will stay out his time here, even if I have to quit the tour for the rest of the year.''

"I'm so glad," Rae said, feeling confident and relieved. "We love him so much." She wanted to say more about Kevin being part of their lives now, perhaps hint that Nick was, too. But she found herself politely dismissed; he said he was going to call his lawyer and quickly got off the line to attend to his son's life and happiness.

The ecstatic hope faded a little as Rae quietly returned the phone to its cradle.

Jan, how wrong you are about this man and his son! How willfully wrong. And why?

She was still thinking about it when Harrison Bowers's voice broke into her musings. "Got a minute, Rae?" She looked up to see him quietly shutting her office door. "I've been thinking since our talk that there might be another solution—maybe you *can* have your cake and eat it, too."

She stared at him, trying to bring her mind back to bank business. What on earth was he talking about?

"You probably know, better than anyone, that banking isn't exactly my first love," he said as he settled himself on one corner of her desk. "Much of my success here has been due to my family's twenty-eight-percent ownership of Coastal stock." She only smiled and he nodded. "I came into banking at my father's insistence."

"I see."

He regarded her thoughtfully for a moment. "But I've learned a lot from you, Rae. And not just about banking."

"Oh?"

"You didn't even get excited about that big offer from Corporate. You thought about what would make you happy and it seems to be remaining here in Dansby."

"I guess you're right," she said.

"I've decided to do what makes me happy and it's not banking. I'm an architectural engineer."

"You're kidding!" she exclaimed in surprise. So what was he doing in banking?

"My father didn't approve," he explained. "More money, more prestige in banking. But now... Textralle Buildings International has offered me a job. I'll be low man on the totem pole there, but I'll be doing what I know and like. And I think this move may make both of us happy. See?"

"See what?" she asked, genuinely puzzled.

"You can have my job. And then when you find Mr. Right—"

"Oh, Harrison, I'm not really looking for a Mr. Right, or a Mr. Wrong either." Almost involuntarily she touched the diamond attached to the pearls at her throat. "I just want to do my job. Stay in one place to raise my boys." She smiled up at him. "I'll miss you. And whether or not I find a Mr. Right, I really hope you find your *Ms.* Right. The lady you settle with will be very fortunate. As for my getting your job..." She registered her doubt in tone and expression.

"You've been handling it very well, even with me in the way," he said, laughing.

"Oh, Harrison!" She gave a wry smile. "Yes, I think I could handle it. But to use another cliché, 'There's many a slip betwixt cup and lip!'"

"No, once the Textralle thing comes through, you're in. That is, unless you refuse."

They talked more about it, she reminding him that a woman had never been chosen as a regional director, he saying there was no one else more suited for the job. If Corporate didn't know this, he did, and surely he—and his twenty-eight percent—had some clout!

"Of course, the other position is still available. I just want you to know that now you have a choice," he concluded. "Think about it."

She did think about it—or as much as she could with another thought dominating her mind. Nick. How wonderful if he could really be part of her life. Because she was in love with him. And she now knew he wasn't involved with Elaine Cummings. She also knew with absolute certainty that he was nothing like Tom. She imagined what it would be like to live with Nick, to be married to him.

But there was many a slip betwixt cup and lip.

CHAPTER FOURTEEN

RAE SPENT A RESTLESS night and was rather bleary-eyed when she reported for work the next morning. She performed her duties diligently but mechanically, with none of her usual zeal. She felt out of sorts, dull, even a little dazed.

A call from a Mr. McKenzie did get her attention, though.

"I just wanted to let you know you can relax," he said. "I've had quite a session with my lawyer and with Jan. Kevin will stay out his time here. Maybe longer if he likes and I can work things out."

The "longer" made her catch her breath. Did that mean...? "I'm so pleased...and relieved," she gasped. "Lady Fraser sounded so...so definite. I was afraid that—"

"That I couldn't pull it off?" He chuckled. "I told you not to worry. In fact I'm glad she made this move. It...well, it rather brought matters to a head. Things will be very different from here on in."

"Oh? I hope that means Kevin will be spending more time with you."

"I hope so. Would you like to hear about it?"

"I certainly would." She spoke in a rush. "Tonight," she said eagerly. "Why don't you come for dinner? About six?"

"No, my place. Would you mind? I'd rather Kevin not hear some of this."

"I understand. I'll come directly from work."

IT SEEMED AS IF everything was working against her just because she wanted to leave early. She was stopped by some request or phone call every time she started out, and it was after six when she finally left the office.

She had called home and made arrangements for the boys, indicating that she'd be at Nick's after seven o'clock. Things seemed to be on an even keel there. Kevin said he'd walk Rusty and pick up Joey from Helen's; Greg was to prepare hamburgers and salad.

She arrived at Nick's place, glanced at his car in the carport and was vividly reminded of the last time she'd been here. Flushed with the heat of memory, she took a deep breath. Things were not as they had seemed.

Her heart skipped a beat as she nervously pressed the bell. Then Nick opened the door and all thought of herself vanished.

He looked tired. She wanted to smooth away the frown lines around his eyes, brush that lock of hair from his forehead. She wanted to put her arms around him and hold him close.

"Did Jan give you a hard time?" she asked.

"It's been more hectic than hard." He smiled. Just seeing her gave him a lift. She looked so trim and smart, dressed for success in that dark-green coatdress. She'd been working all day, but she looked as fresh as if she'd just stepped from a shower. Fresh, pretty—and damned provocative! No one would guess she was reserved to a fault. *Or maybe just reserved with me,* he thought resignedly as he gestured toward the sofa. "Sit and relax and let me get you a cold drink. I make a mean daiquiri. Want to try it?"

She nodded. "Anything." Just being with him was enough. Almost enough. He went into the kitchen and she picked up a magazine from the coffee table and thumbed through it, seeing nothing. She reminded herself that she was a full-grown woman—so she would act like one. She would be composed, sophisticated and... how did one act alluring?

Nick returned and handed her a frosted glass filled to the brim with a colorful mixture of strawberries, vodka, crushed ice and she wasn't sure what else. "Delicious," she said as she tried it.

"Thanks." He set the tray with the half-filled decanter on the coffee table and took up his own glass. "I need this more than you do," he remarked as he sat beside her and stretched out his legs. "I've had a hell of a day. I meant to cook for you, but since we talked I've been busy arguing with my lawyer, my accountant and the PGA secretary about canceling the next event. So I hope you'll settle for a gourmet pizza I've taken the liberty of ordering."

"Of course." Food was the last thing on her mind. "And Jan? You've come to an amicable agreement?"

He grinned at her. "You sound doubtful."

"Oh, no," she said hastily. "But I know—I mean, I get the impression that she can be..." Rae bit her tongue. Spiteful, vindictive, mean as hell! "Somewhat uncooperative," she finished.

Nick laughed, almost choking on his drink. "So you've experienced her sharp tongue, have you? You ought to hear her when she really takes off her gloves. I admit she's pretty furious, but in this case, helpless. I'm applying for sole custody of Kevin. My solicitor thinks I'll get it now that he's old enough to voice his preference. I think I know what that choice will be—

thanks to this year and to you," he added, lifting his glass to her.

"Not me. You. Once he got to know you. I don't understand how you let that woman—" She broke off.

"She *is* his mother." He refilled both their glasses. "But that wasn't the only reason." While they sipped their drinks he told her. His own travel and forced absences had made it impossible for him to provide Kevin with a stable home; as well, there was good schooling available in London and an endless number of cultural opportunities—theater, music, libraries—though Kevin seemed to prefer the summers at his grandfather's farm. "And now that Kevin is older," he concluded, "I mean to see that he makes his own choices. Which is one reason I wanted to talk with you tonight. They've offered him a full-time job at the vet school this summer and he's eager to accept. He even hinted that he might prefer to finish high school here instead of returning to his school in England. Well, I still travel a great deal and he's still young and—"

She put her hand over his. "You don't need to ask. Kevin is like my own son. He can stay with us as long as he likes."

"Thanks, Rae. I think being with you has been the best thing that has happened for him. And for me too. It gave us a chance to get to know each other, brought us close enough to talk things out and make decisions together. How can I ever repay you?"

"You might try another daiquiri," she said, blushing with pleasure at his words.

"Coming right up." He picked up the empty decanter.

She felt like she was on a cloud, floating with joy, as she watched him retreat to the kitchen. Kevin would not be leaving. And neither would Nick. But if she took the job at Corporate and moved to L.A., would they move with her? Anywhere there was a golf course... Her thoughts whirred dizzily in tune with Nick's mixer. She'd talk it over with him, delighted that she could do so, now that they were on a friendly footing again.

"There's something else we'd better discuss," she said when he returned with the drinks.

"Oh?"

"I've been offered another job." She kicked off her pumps, curled her feet under her, and told him all about it.

"Do you want this job?" he asked bluntly.

"In a way." She sipped her drink thoughtfully. "It would be a challenge. I'm worried about the boys, though." She voiced her concerns. "But Harrison thinks I may be blackballed from any advancement if I don't take it."

Nick seemed to stiffen. "Harrison?"

"Mr. Bowers. My boss."

"I know who he is." Nick set his glass down hard. "Is he also moving to L.A.?"

"Harrison?" she asked, puzzled. Was Nick glaring at her? She shook her head as much to clear it as to answer his question. "No. Though he *will* be moving."

"But not with you?" He seemed to put a great deal of emphasis on the question.

"Oh, no. He's moving to a new job—in an entirely different field." For some reason it struck her as funny and she began to giggle as she told him what Bowers had said. "He thinks I could get *his* job. But I—"

"Never mind all that. If you and Bowers aren't—Never mind," he said again. He took her glass and placed it on the table, then held both her hands in his.

"Just tell me one thing, Rae. Why did you leave me that day in Monterey?"

"I..." She hesitated, taken aback by the abruptness of the question. "I told you. The bank."

"No. It was during the holidays and you had arranged a week's leave. Tell me the truth. You owe me that."

She drew her hands away and shook her head. She didn't *want* him to know the truth.

"It's all right," he said gently. "If you really don't care for me—"

"But I do!" She looked up at him, eyes wide. She felt befuddled, not quite herself, and she desperately needed to hold fast to the closeness she'd just begun to recapture. She couldn't stand for him to think she didn't care! The words tumbled out. "I care more than you know." Her voice dropped to a whisper. "I may be...I—I love you." The words were scarcely audible but he must have heard, for he pulled her gently into his arms, holding her as if he'd never let her go.

"As much as I love you?" he asked, his lips against her temple, caressing, warming, exciting.

"More." She felt a surge of *joy*, elation. "More than I ever thought it possible to love anyone."

"So tell me, love, why have we wasted all this time? Why did you abandon me that day in Monterey?"

She shook her head, hiding her face against his chest.

"Trust me, love," he coaxed.

"I was scared," she whispered.

"Of me?" He sounded incredulous.

"No. Of me." She sat up, moved away from him. It would be best to tell him before...before they... But once he knew, would he still want her? She picked up her half-finished drink and took several swallows. "The truth is I'm not... I can't... I'm not very sexy."

She ran a finger around the rim of the glass, not looking at him.

"I see." He spoke quietly, sounding very solemn. "I assume you've divined this through your vast experience?"

"Please don't make this harder." She gazed at him through a blur of unkind memories. "I couldn't please my husband."

"Oh? Did he please you?"

"I don't know." She had never thought about that. "I—I don't remember. I don't know much about... about sex." Only that she'd been a dismal failure and her husband had sought happiness and satisfaction from other women. She almost choked as she took a swallow of the now-warm daiquiri—which had contributed immensely to her now-loose tongue. "I was so ashamed. I've never told anyone, not even my mother, but Tom had asked for a divorce. The very day before his heart attack. He was going to marry someone else." Beautiful, vivacious, *sexy* Leslie Powers. "A woman who was...was everything I'm not."

"I see." His intent gaze made her uncomfortable. This was hard, but she had to be fair.

"I failed Tom," she said, keeping her voice steady. She drew a deep breath and looked up at him. "That day at the inn... Oh, Nick, I couldn't bear to fail you. That was why I left."

"I see."

It was as if she was wrapped in a cocoon of misery and there was no escape. She remained where she was, feet still curled under her. Well, she'd told him.

Just then he bent and kissed her, his lips lingering against hers. "I love you," he whispered. "Will you marry me?"

She stared at him. "Didn't you hear me? I'm—"

"Did you hear me?" He cupped her face in his hands, kissed her again so tenderly, so possessively, that a tremor of desire raced through her. "We've wasted enough time, my love. I want you to be mine—and soon. Will you?"

"Yes, oh yes." A burst of pleasure shot through her, blotting out all other thought. To be his wife, to belong to him, to have him belong to her. She hardly heard the peal of the doorbell.

"I think our dinner has arrived," he said. He touched a finger to her cheek and fished bills out of his pocket as he started toward the door. He returned, bearing a pizza, and the spicy smells wafting from it made Rae realize she was ravenously hungry.

"What's this hot-wheels competition Joey keeps talking about?" Nick asked as he served pizza and poured coffee.

"Oh, that's one of the Cub Scout projects. They make these cars and race them against each other."

"I see. One of these model things you get in a package?"

"No, not at all. You have to make it from scratch. I think it's permissible to buy the little wheels and things like that at a hardware store, but you have to carve the car out of a block of wood and—"

"You're kidding! And Joey expects me to help him!" He looked so shocked that Rae laughed. And felt much better. The food and coffee were having an immediate effect. Sobering. Refreshing.

Throughout the meal, Nick kept talking about these personal but impersonal things. The conversation made Rae feel relaxed and comfortable. It was a joyful feeling—slightly diminished by a hovering cloud of apprehension. Had he really understood what she'd said? Would she fail him as she had failed Tom? No. Not when all she wanted was to make him happy.

When they were finished, she swung her feet to the floor and started to gather up the dishes.

"No, you don't." Nick pulled her back onto the sofa. "We need to talk, my love."

Now. Warily, she moved a little away from him.

"Don't run. This is tell-the-truth day and I want you close to me when we face facts." He chuckled as he pulled her against him and kissed the top of her head. "Remember I once told you that you've got the super-woman syndrome?"

"Yes." How could she forget it? That was the day they'd had that knock-down drag-out argument over his letting the boys go up on the roof.

"I told you then that nobody's perfect."

She sat up straight and drew back from him. "I never said I was perfect!"

"All right. So you didn't. Now let's talk about your perfections." He turned her toward him. "I want to see your face when I tell you why I love you."

"Oh, Nick. You do love me? Still?" She searched his face, afraid to discover a flicker of doubt.

"Still. Isn't it amazing?" He gave a dramatic sigh. "I'm trying to figure it out. There's no doubt you're a perfect mother, but that benefits the children, not me. A top banker, too. This new job offer proves it. Which reminds me—" He looked suddenly serious. "Do you want to take that job?"

"Job?" It was the last thing on her mind at this moment.

"The one in L.A. Your main concern seems to be how your taking it would affect the boys."

She nodded vaguely.

"We could arrange things, you know. We could live wherever you like. I could easily curtail my tournaments so that I'd always be with the boys when you travel."

She regarded him with awe. "You'd really do that? Move wherever I want? Cut down on your tournaments?"

"Of course." He seemed puzzled that this surprised her.

She wrapped her arms around him and kissed him over and over again. "Do you know what I think? I think you're the most wonderful man in the entire world. And I wouldn't take a job that would often drag me away from you and my boys. And I don't want you to curtail your tours. I love to see you play and I want to be the one who kisses you when you win or lose! I want . . . I want to stay right here in Dansby whether I get Harrison's job or not." She stopped as she felt tears spring to her eyes. "Oh, Nick, I'm so happy. And scared. I don't know why you love me. I'm not—"

He stopped her protest with a kiss that sent a warm delicious tremor rippling through her. She was sorry when he drew his lips away.

"Let me count the reasons I love you. For one thing, you make me laugh. Do you know how witty you are? You come out with the best quips at the most unexpected moments. I like your sense of humor. You're quite the dancer, too. Didn't we have fun that night?"

She nodded, unable to speak. He was whispering, his lips lightly touching her ear, making her feel all quivery inside.

"Yes," she gasped, as he transferred his lips to that frantic pulse beating in her throat. "You're sensitive to others' needs, too. You spotted Kevin's problem right away. It never occurred to me that he was afraid of not measuring up to a famous dad. You're a very perceptive, sensitive, warm-hearted woman. I love that about you." His caressing hands were creating a peculiar tightening in her stomach.

"Oh, Nick, I..." she whispered, reaching up to tangle her fingers in his hair and pull his lips to hers.

"Of course, we'll have to talk about this *cold fish* business." The tone was light and teasing but the words made her shudder.

"Don't! Don't joke about it." She had to make him face her problem. Even if it ruined everything. "You need to understand, Nick. Perhaps to rethink this whole thing. I am...Tom...Tom said I was just one of those frigid women. Oh, stop it!" she protested as he waved his hands in complete dismissal of her concerns. "I can't believe you're taking it so lightly."

"And I can't believe you've been harboring such an absurd idea for so long. Or that you never once doubted your ex." Then, sounding more serious, he looked down at her. "Haven't you heard? There are no frigid women, only men who are poor lovers."

She stared at him, speechless. No, she'd never heard that. Had never doubted Tom. Had never even discussed this with anyone. But then, there'd been no need. There had been no man in her life until now.

"It's a well-established fact according to dozens of experts in the field." He quirked an eyebrow. "Ever consulted one?"

"Never."

He clicked his tongue and gave his head a disparaging shake. "Never mind, love. We'll learn together."

A moment later he was kissing her with a tender demanding passion that sent a voracious hunger surging through her. A new yearning that urged, that promised, that banished all doubt.